The night's traumatic events, the personal violation she had suffered at the hands of the kidnappers, the loving care and protection Ben provided for her despite her stubborn hardheadedness, the thoughts and emotions tumbled around in Maribeth's mind and she began to cry again.

Ben stroked her face, kissed her eyes and cheeks, murmured softly to her as sobs shook her.

"You're safe, my love, and trust me, I'll see that you are always safe from now on."

"Oh, Ben, I was so scared!"

"I know, honey, I know."

It was a night neither would forget. As Maribeth lay secure in Ben's arms that night she understood with sudden clarity that although she had always thought she wanted total independence and the freedom to make her own decisions, pursue her own goals, there came a time in a woman's life, if she was lucky, when she would find her partner, the other half that made her whole.

She snuggled closer to Ben, who lay sleeping beside her. The solid warmth of his firm, muscular body assured her that she was *very* lucky. She was loved by a good man and she loved him.

Half asleep, Ben sensed Maribeth was awake and drew her closer. He kissed her forehead and murmured, "I've waited so long to have you here beside me. Now I *know* you're safe. You're here with me, my love."

"And it's where I want to be, Ben. I love you, Ben. Guess I always have, just too hardheaded to understand . . ."

"I love you, too, my Maribeth. Have since the day I saw you at the hospital. An angel if ever I saw one," he whispered.

Maribeth answered with a kiss that led to a beginning they never wanted to end.

BOOK YOUR PLACE ON OUR WEBSITE AND MAKE THE ARABESQUE ROMANCE CONNECTION!

We've created a customized website just for our very special Arabesque readers, where you can get the inside scoop on everything that's going on with Arabesque romance novels.

When you come online, you'll have the exciting opportunity to:

- View covers of upcoming books

- Learn about our future publishing schedule (listed by publication month and author)

- Find out when your favorite authors will be visiting a city near you

- Search for and order backlist books

- Check out author bios and background information

- Send e-mail to your favorite authors

- Join us in weekly chats with authors, readers and other guests

- Get writing guidelines

- AND MUCH MORE!

Visit our website at
http://www.arabesquebooks.com

MEANT TO BE

Mildred Riley

ARABESQUE
BET
BOOKS

BET Publications, LLC
http://www.bet.com
http://www.arabesquebooks.com

ARABESQUE BOOKS are published by

BET Publications, LLC
c/o BET BOOKS
One BET Plaza
1900 W Place NE
Washington, DC 20018-1211

Copyright © 2003 by Mildred Riley

All rights reserved. No part of this book may be reproduced, stored in a retrieval system, or transmitted in any form or by any means without the prior written consent of the Publisher.

If you purchased this book without a cover, you should be aware that this book is stolen property. It was reported as "unsold and destroyed" to the Publisher and neither the Author nor the Publisher has received any payment for this "stripped book."

All Kensington Titles, Imprints and Distributed Lines are available at special quantity discounts for bulk purchases for sales promotions, premiums, fund-raising, and educational or institutional use. Special book excerpts or customized printings can also be created to fit specific needs. For details, write or phone the office of the Kensington special sales manager: Kensington Publishing Corp., 850 Third Avenue, New York, NY 10022, attn. Special Sales Department, Phone: 1-800-221-2647.

BET BOOKS is a trademark of Black Entertainment Television, Inc. ARABESQUE, the ARABESQUE logo, and the BET BOOKS logo are trademarks and registered trademarks.

First printing: August 2003
10 9 8 7 6 5 4 3 2 1

Printed in the United States of America

*In memory of Maria,
whose life enriched my own in so many ways.*

Prologue

Bernie Hazzard's teeth ached, always a bad sign for him. They hurt even worse after tonight's fight against Tim Sippowicz. Bernie's trainer-manager, Roscoe Dunlap, had warned him about his opponent's reputation as a clever fighter.

"The kid's quick with his combinations, but, Bernie, you got speed *and* power . . . use it so he can't work his combos. Keep crowdin' him so he can't get 'em at you."

But it *had* been one of the combinations that Bernie never saw coming. He had landed a solid right to Tim's body and connected with a left when Tim suddenly moved left. He hit Bernie with a quick left jab and a right cross followed by a left hook to the jaw that had Bernie reeling when mercifully the bell sounded and the round ended. Bernie stumbled to his corner. Roscoe pushed the weary warrior down on the stool. He poured cold water over Bernie's head and neck. The cut man looked Bernie over carefully to tend to any cuts and bruises. He wiped Bernie's blistering hot face, applied grease while Roscoe ranted and raved at his stunned fighter.

"What's the matter with you, kid? You got to pick

up! You can't let this guy win this fight! Don't you want this fight, huh? Huh?"

He shoved his face close to Bernie's and in a low voice spoke into his fighter's ear.

"*Do* what you gotta do! Okay?"

He slapped Bernie briskly on the face as the bell sounded for the start of the next round.

"Okay?" Roscoe shouted.

Bernie nodded numbly, but somehow he realized that he had lost the fight. It had been five tough rounds and Bernie knew he had met a better, more skillful boxer than he was.

He had started out his day at five in the morning when he got up to haul his father's fresh farm vegetables, tomatoes, corn, and squash to Haymarket Square. After delivering the produce, he stopped for coffee. He dared not have any doughnuts because of the fight that night. He had to watch his weight, which was difficult for him. His trainer always warned him not to eat the day of a fight.

"A hungry fighter is a mean fighter! Remember that, Bernie!"

Earlier, when he left home that morning, his father had asked him when he would be back home.

"Afta you drop off the produce . . . or when?" his father had asked.

"Nah, Pa, got this fight for tonight. Be at the gym doin' some sparrin', then rest before the fight. Gotta see Roscoe, too, settle on some things."

"Be home later, eh?"

"Afta twelve, but I'll be up at five to get the stuff to market. Don't worry, Pa, just have the produce ready n' I'll load the truck."

Bernie didn't know that he was going to go to the hospital. It was almost eleven when he found himself driving past it, feeling the most miserable pain he'd ever felt after a match. Usually he felt achy from the bruises and battering of his body from his opponent's blows, but tonight it was more than being fight weary. His body felt numb, especially his arms and legs. And his face, particularly his teeth, jaw, head, and ears, all felt as if a strange numbness had come over him.

Impulsively, he braked the truck to a halt and ran, stumbling blindly almost, his vision suddenly impaired. He ran across the street to the front of the building. He didn't know why he parked the truck on this street instead of in front of the building. There were plenty of parking spaces. Subconsciously, he seemed to feel the need to flee from the confined cab of the truck. He knew he needed relief from his awful distress. Somewhere inside that darkened building there should be someone who would know how to ease his tormenting pain. Now he heard a fierce ringing in his ears, profound dizziness, and sudden, overwhelming weakness in his legs.

He continued to try to run up the smooth granite stairs. A wave of nausea came over him. He stumbled and fell. Flickering stabs of starlights pricked at his eyeballs as he faltered and plummeted face forward.

For as along as Maribeth could remember, the established ritual for the Trumbull family, Emily and Judd and their only child, Maribeth, was a large Sunday dinner. Usually it was a substantial roast beef, pork, chicken, or often Mr. Trumbull's favorite, a leg of lamb. There would be rice and peas, gravy, a green vegetable, possibly string beans, salad made with sliced cucumbers and tomatoes, always freshly made yeast rolls with plenty of butter, condiments such as chutney, mint, or cranberry sauce, depending on the meat served. Dessert was quite often a chocolate layer cake, coconut cake, even fruitcake if the meal was near the holiday season.

When Judd Trumbull had married Emily DeVries he told her, "You'll keep me at your beck n' call long's you cook a big Sunday dinner."

She had assured him that his request would be no problem for her.

This particular Sunday Maribeth, a newly graduated registered nurse, still living with her parents, was on her way up to her room to study or possibly take a nap before she reported to work for her eleven-to-seven night-duty assignment.

Her father watched her leave from his chair in the living room. He placed on the floor the portion of the Sunday paper he'd been reading.

"Look, Maribeth, I'm goin' take your car out, check it over, get gas and oil n' such. Think I'll check the tires, too, an' anythin' else that needs checkin'."

"Gee, thanks, Dad. So far I haven't had any trouble. Car's running just fine."

"Well, I aim to keep it that way. It's an old car, got to work at keeping her runnin', you know."

"I know. Thanks, Dad."

Judd Trumbull returned home about an hour and a half later. Maribeth had finished studying and returned to help her mother finishing up the dishes from their Sunday meal.

Her father burst through the door, almost

MEANT TO BE 11

breathless, as if he had been running from someone or something.

The two women stared at him as he blurted out, "We're at war! The Japs just bombed Pearl Harbor!"

"Where's Pearl Harbor?" Maribeth asked.

"War? My God, Judd," her mother said, "are you sure?"

"It's all over the radio!" He ran into the living room, the women following on his heels as he turned on the RCA console radio on the table beside his big chair.

"Listen!"

A male announcer's voice was reporting that at seven fifty-five Hawaii time that morning the Japanese had attacked Pearl Harbor. His voice crackled with both static and emotion as he related the events. The attack lasted two hours, he said. The president, Franklin Roosevelt, had been notified and was expected to respond with a message to Congress the next day declaring that the country was at war.

The stunned family stood staring transfixedly at the simple wooden box, at the dire message it sent that instantly changed their lives.

Emily Trumbull stared at her husband, worry creases lining her troubled, usually serene face.

"Judd, will . . . will you have to serve? Will they call you up?" she worried.

"I don't think so, sweetheart. I'm too old, I think."

"Oh, thank God!" Her eyes filled with tears. "Maybe because you are in night school and working at the shipyard . . ."

"I'm still only an apprentice, you know," he reminded his wife.

He put his arm around his worried wife and pulled Maribeth close with his other arm.

"We'll get through this, some kinda way," he said. "We'll have to trust in the Lord."

Standing in the middle of the living room with her parents' arms around her, Maribeth had a sense of security that she knew they wanted to give her, but what did the future hold for her, for her family, for her country?

The daily newspapers the next morning screamed the headline U.S. AT WAR! Maribeth read the horrendous litany of over two thousand navy casualties, several hundred marine, army, and civilian deaths, twenty-one ships sunk, over one hundred aircraft destroyed. She could hardly believe what she was reading.

That day, December 8, the president addressed a joint session of Congress. It was a short talk that took him only six minutes to read. He declared, "Yesterday, December seventh, 1941, is a day that will live in infamy." Maribeth read a comment from one of the president's secretaries, *The president has maintained greater outward calm than anyone else, but there was rage in his very calm.*

Maribeth felt the same way.

One

She would be happy when this awful war came to an end. She longed for peace and for life to be the way it was before that fateful day in December a few years back. Since then the scarcity of food, clothing, gasoline, everything that she was accustomed to having, had been rationed—sent to the boys fighting in Europe and the Pacific. Even doctors and nurses were in short supply. Most of the able-bodied ones had joined up with medical and surgical units overseas. Those remaining stateside were newly graduated doctors and nurses—plus doctors too old to serve.

It was, she thought, almost like being in limbo, half alive—this waiting for the war to end. Maribeth couldn't wait for the lights to come on again. She hated the blackout, but it was vitally necessary. She had to live with it. Everyone did. The enemy might try to invade, God forbid.

Maribeth Trumbull peered through her car's windshield into the inky darkness. She drove slowly down Seaver Street onto Columbus Avenue toward Ruggles Street. Because the war was at its height and gasoline was rationed, she had to drive under forty miles an hour. She knew it would take about a half hour to reach her destination. It was only because she was a nurse and worked the night tour of duty that she was out at all. She was just about to make a left turn when a shadowy figure veered suddenly in her car's headlights. All she saw was white socks floating, disembodied, near the ground.

"Oh God!" she whispered. She slammed on her brakes. She had missed the drunk by inches.

She was still badly shaken by the time she reached Zion Memorial Hospital. She sat for a few minutes in the dimly lit parking lot, her breathing finally slowed to a normal rate and her nerves calmed somewhat. She noticed the red lighted sign that pointed the way to the emergency room. *Dear God, if I had hit that man, I'd be on my way in there,* she thought.

She sat still for a moment. Then sighing, she reached for the shoe box that held her white organdy nurse's cap, picked up her red sweater and her flashlight and purse. As she headed up the granite steps of the hospital's main entrance she heard a low moan. She swept the beam of her flashlight over the wide stairway. To her left, on the top of the landing, she saw what looked like a pile of dark clothing. As she got closer she saw a black heavy sweater, dark trousers curved into a fetal position. Her light revealed more. She saw a man's hand, pale, bluish white, and a stark-white face, wide blue eyes that stared up at her. There was white froth around the man's open mouth and a distinct odor, like burned flesh. A seizure? she thought. She raced into the hospital.

"There's a patient on the front steps!" she informed the switchboard operator, the only person on duty in the lobby. "You'd better notify security."

"Wait, wait!" the operator called after Maribeth,

who was halfway down the corridor to the nursing office. She had to sign in and get to her assigned case to relieve the shift nurse. Even with all that had happened tonight, she did not want to be late. As a member of a minority, she couldn't afford a blemish on her reputation of not being dependable. It was important to her that she always report for duty on time.

Maribeth saw Ben's eyes narrow as he peered at her over the mug of hot coffee she had just handed him. He swallowed a mouthful of the liquid, put his cup down quietly on the coffee table between them, and glared intently at her. Maribeth knew he was upset.

"I've never, ever met a woman as stubborn as you, Maribeth Trumbull! Don't you know how much I worry about you—driving that old tin can, and at night!" he argued.

"What's wrong with my car? Gets me where I want to go, thank you," she said as she bit into her Spam sandwich. Meat was hard to come by with the war at its height, and they often shared a quick snack before going on their individual night jobs; hers at the hospital and his at the local precinct station.

"Well, I still worry about you driving alone, like I said, at night in a car that's not in the best condition. You could break down anywhere. In the blackout we have in the city now, so few streetlights around, anything could happen to you alone like that."

"Don't worry, Ben," Maribeth insisted. "I can take care of myself—"

"That's what you think," he interrupted. "It's a

mad, crazy world out there. Don't know why . . ." he started to say. He shook his head, took a seat beside her on the sofa.

"Listen, my friend," Maribeth said, "I've already made up my mind that I'm getting my college degree, come hell or high water, and the only way I can do it is to work night duty. So that's what I'm going to do."

Ben sought to appease Maribeth. "But, honey, you *know* how I feel about you. I don't want to discourage you, but you know I want us to get married. I've got a good job with the police department and I want to take care of you."

Ben shook his head with a sidelong glance at the young woman whose loveliness had captivated him the minute she came into the emergency room at Zion Memorial Hospital to check on the prisoner he was guarding. The patient was whining and groaning about his broken leg that he'd sustained in a stolen car accident. Tall, slender, cool, and professional, Maribeth Trumbull went about her nursing duties with only the barest acknowledgment of the police officer. For his part, Ben was stunned by her beauty. Her starched-white uniform did not hide long legs, encased in white, nor her small waist above which rose delicate outlines of her well-proportioned breasts. Her creamy, softly tanned coloring was enhanced by her red-brown hair made even more attractive by the small white organdy nurse's cap she wore. Ben watched, bewitched, as she went about her nursing responsibilities, checking the patient's still wet cast that had been applied.

"Wiggle your toes, please, sir," she instructed the patient.

MEANT TO BE 17

She examined the man's bruises, which had been treated.

"The doctor will be in to discharge the patient soon," she told Ben. "The cast is almost dry, and he'll be given crutches so he can walk."

Speechless, Ben could only nod, but from that moment he knew he wanted to know this young woman better. He had been seeing her as often as he could. Next Sunday would be special. He'd been invited to dinner at her parents' home in Cambridge. Ben was not certain of Maribeth's feelings toward him. Oh, she was friendly, but for himself, he had fallen in love.

"Look, Ben," she said now, "I know you've always had to be tough and hard-nosed to make it on the police force, but do you *always* have to be so dictatorial? I take care of my car, give it gas, oil, and water, what else does it need?"

"As a nurse, Maribeth, you know . . . just like you have to take care of your body," he chided, "you got to take care of your car. It's a machine, too."

Serious worry lines creased his broad forehead as he pleaded his case.

"It's not the point of *you* taking care of me, Ben, can't you see? I need to know I can take care of myself. I just know you've heard Billie Holiday's 'God Bless the Child.' It's very important to me that I accomplish something that *I* set out to do. What's the point in living if you can't reach your goals?"

"You don't understand, my love. I'm supposed to take care of the woman I love, worry about her—"

"Who says?" Maribeth challenged.

"I do. As a man, I'm supposed to do that."

"Not in my book, Ben. I say women should be

equal, able to make decisions, able to take care of themselves, especially if the need arises."

She stared at Ben, who was shaking his head, a quizzical smile on his face.

"What's the matter with you, Ben? You know there's a war on and women are helping out. They aren't going to sit home and just wait for their husbands and boyfriends to come home from the front. Already they have women working at the Watertown Arsenal and the Boston Naval Shipyard making guns, building ships, and, yes, making decisions, too. I tell you, my dear Ben." She smiled softly. "They are not going to be the quiet 'dear, take care of me' women that the men left behind. I, for one, have the feeling that once they get it, most women are not going to give up their independence. Not easily, that is."

"I still say you are the most hardheaded, stubborn, strong-minded woman I ever met, but . . ." Ben moved closer to Maribeth on the couch, put his arm around her, and tilted back her head with his forefinger. Over her head he murmured softly, "I love every stubborn, obstinate, tough bone in your precious body." Impulsively, he kissed her lightly and held her close. Maribeth pulled back to look at him.

"So, you'll stop hounding me about my working nights and going to school?" she asked.

"Hounding you, yes. But worrying about you, no, and don't you forget that."

"Long's you keep your worries to yourself, my good friend," Maribeth conceded.

"Will do. But promise me you'll take no chances, watch your back, and call me whenever you need me. All right?"

MEANT TO BE

"Right, boss." Maribeth smiled and snapped off a two-fingered salute at her concerned friend.

"Maribeth," Ben continued, bringing his thoughts back to the present, "you know with the war goin' on, an' nobody knows how long it's goin' to last, car parts are already hard to come by. That's why you have to take care of your car, even if it is old. A tune-up, an oil change, lube job ever so often, not only will she run better, she'll last longer," he argued. "Be glad to help you out—"

Maribeth flicked her hand on Ben's arm, interrupting his offer. She wanted to allay his fears. "My dad's already warned me about car parts, and I don't need your money, Ben, but if it will ease your worried mind any, I'll take the car to my dad's mechanic in Cambridge on my next day off. You and my dad, you're one of a kind," she sighed.

"Well, it would make me feel better, with you driving to the hospital at night. You know I don't want anything to happen to you. And another thing," he added, "you have enough gas ration coupons? I know as a nurse you should have, but if you run short, you let me know, okay? I know three gallons a week is not much."

"Yes, sir!" Maribeth teased.

Secretly, though, she had not indicated her growing interest in the young police officer. She was pleased that he cared about her safety. She glanced covertly in his direction. She had to admit to herself that she delighted in the tall, muscular leanness of his body, what she called his "noble" head, with close-cropped dark, smooth hair. When she had first described him to her mother, she said, "Mama, he is *fine* looking! Finest I've seen in a long time. And believe me, I've seen 'em all; short, fat, bowlegged, bald, pimply-faced, never knew people could look so bad . . ."

"Well, if they're sick, guess they would look bad when you see them."

"Course, you're right there, Mama, but really, it's more than Ben's looks. It's his way, his manner. He's sure of himself, quiet, takes no nonsense, no stuff from anybody."

Her mother had smiled indulgently at her only child, pleased to see her daughter finally interested in a nice young man. So many eligible men were overseas.

"You really like him, don't you, honey?"

"Yes, Mama, I do. He's a lot like Daddy—knows what he wants and won't be satisfied until he gets it."

She remembered the childhood incident that indicated what kind of father she really had. She had gone home from school that day, dreading to face her parents. Her mother was scrubbing clothes.

"You're goin' to have to tell your father as soon as he wakes up. That's all there is to it!"

Standing over the washtub, Maribeth's mother had slapped a wet towel on the washboard, demonstrating her strong response to her daughter's announcement. With great, furious strokes, she scrubbed the towel on the board. Maribeth watched, felt the thrumming noise reverberate with the tumultuous beating of her own heart. She knew her mother was angered by her news, but she knew, too, that her father's anger would be worse. He was the parent with the white-hot temper, and everyone knew it.

"Tell me again what your teacher said?" her mother questioned as she continued to pound the towel on the washboard. "Said . . . my family was poor, my father couldn't afford to send me to college . . . so it didn't make sense for me to sign up for the college course in high school anyway. She said I was going to end up being a maid, so the general course was good enough."

"She said that?"

Maribeth nodded.

Maribeth's mother straightened her weary back, pushed her tangled hair out of her eyes with a wet hand, and sighed. "What did you say, honey, when she said that?"

"Told her I still wanted to go to college, be a teacher someday . . ."

"Good! What'd she have to say to *that*?"

"Said nobody, no school board that she knows of hires colored teachers. That my best chance for a job was in domestic service."

"The witch!" Emily Trumbull slapped the heavy wet towel against the washboard again. "Some white woman's kitchen, she means! Damn woman don't know who she's dealin' with! Don't know Judd Trumbull! But sure as sin she's goin' find out! Yes, ma'am, that . . . Miss Perkins, you say her name is?"

Again Maribeth nodded.

"Well, she's 'bout to meet one provoked, worked-up island man! White folks like her have their way, we'll never amount to anything."

"Miss Perkins did say with my looks and my quiet manners anybody would be glad to have me work for them. I'd always have a job, she said—"

"What's your looks got to do with it?" her mother interrupted angrily. "She means just because you're light-skinned. Well, your father and I not raisin' you to be in nobody's kitchen! No matter what that Miss Perkins thinks! You go 'head now, change your clothes, honey, so we can get supper on the table. We'll talk about what we're goin' do, after. I'm so mad right now, wouldn't take me but a minute to put a hex on that white woman! Put the fear of God into her. But don't worry, honey, I'll be nice. Don't want to shame you. You keep on studying, getting good marks, and if it takes every penny we can scratch hold of, you're goin' to college . . . if that's what you want."

Maribeth saw the red flush on her mother's face and knew it was not only from her anger at Maribeth's humiliating experience, but the strenuous ordeal of scrubbing dirty clothes as well. Another reason why Maribeth wanted to please her hard-working parents.

Emily DeVries had come to Boston from New Orleans to leave a soured relationship behind. When she met the young, handsome, brown-skinned Jamaican Judd Trumbull, she knew she had found real love. Judd frequently reminded Emily, in his lilting, delightful accent, "Girl mine, you always be the love of my life. That's why God sent this hard-headed, scrabble-down creature to the new worl', so's I could fin' me better half." He promised his lovely dark-eyed, copper-colored Emily that she'd have the best the world had to offer, but with his work as a day laborer with few job skills, his little family was forever only a few dollars away from dire poverty. Deeply in love with his beautiful Emily, Judd managed to get a job as an apprentice at the naval shipyard. Eager to do better, he enrolled in night classes at the local high school. His early youth, working in cane fields in Jamaica, prepared him for hard work. Ambition to improve his lot and

MEANT TO BE

that of his family glowed within him like a white-hot furnace.

Emily knew what Judd would say when he learned of his only child's humiliating experience. He would be angry, but as always would temper his emotion with a verse from Ecclesiastes: for gold is tried in the fire and acceptable men in the fire of adversity. Then he would set out to change, make right whatever it was that plagued him. He always seemed fortified by his faith. She hoped this latest news about their only child wouldn't upset him too much—she'd wait and see.

Emily Trumbull wrung out the last few pieces of washing and placed the wet bundles on the drain board of the sink. She dragged the washtub of dirty water to the kitchen back door and emptied it on the porch floor. She used a broom to sweep the water away. Then she hung the galvanized washtub and washboard on nails attached to the wall of the house.

When she reentered the house, she glanced at the clock on the wall. Four-thirty. She'd have to have supper ready soon so Judd could eat at five and get to his six o'clock class.

The nerve of that teacher telling Maribeth she'd make a good domestic, when the child scarcely had to lift a finger at home. Emily thought of her own pampered childhood in New Orleans. Delray and Antoinette DeVries were of Creole stock and would be distressed if they knew of their beautiful daughter's circumstances. Emily DeVries Trumbull often thought about her parents, but after the failed relationship, one that they had encouraged, Emily fled New Orleans, family, and her past to find fulfilling happiness with Judd and their child. She never told Judd about the indulgent, gracious life she had been accustomed to; merely accepted his love, admired and cared for him and their child.

Sarah Perkins looked up, disapprovingly, from her desk in the eighth grade classroom. Who were these colored people? Then she recognized Maribeth Trumbull, one of her students, and surmised that the two colored adults were her parents.

The man was slender, medium height, with a quick alertness about him. He seemed to take in everything in the classroom at once. His skin was deep brown, smooth, and unlined. He wore a pencil-line dark mustache, was well groomed, although Sarah Perkins could see his clothes were his Sunday best. Maribeth's mother, she could see, was most attractive. Her skin was a copper, reddish brown, enhanced by almost ebony dark eyes. She could see where Maribeth got her good looks. *For Negroes, they are an attractive family,* she admitted to herself.

"Yes, Maribeth, what is it?" she asked.

She noticed the straightforward manner with which the family entered the classroom. Maribeth spoke up.

"These are my parents, Mr. and Mrs. Trumbull," she said formally. "They just want to talk to you. This is Miss Perkins, my homeroom teacher," she told her folks.

Judd Trumbull, hat in hand, nodded. His wife did the same.

"Miss Perkins," he said formally.

"Mr. and Mrs. Trumbull, it's not often students'

parents make a school visit," the teacher said, wondering about the reason for this visit.

Maribeth knew she meant colored parents.

"School has not officially started for the day. You see, I just happen to like to come early," Miss Perkins continued.

"So sorry, I know, Miss . . ."

Sarah Perkins noticed with some astonishment the precise West Indian accent in Judd Trumbull's voice. She sat up straighter behind her desk. A frission of fear skittered down her spine. What *did* these people want with her?

"I told my daughter"—he pronounced it *darter*—"I told her we should be early to straighten out this misunderstanding, be here before the class recite the pledge of allegiance to the flag. You know, *one* nation under God, with liberty and justice for all," he said pointedly. "Wouldn't want to disrupt anyt'ing, but we, her mother and I, need to straighten a few t'ings out. As I see it, you are the teacher, you teach, but you don't have the right to decide our family affairs."

Sarah Perkins's face reddened. What was the man talking about?

"Why, whatever do you mean, *family affairs?*"

"I t'ink you know. You advised my child here to take a general course in high school when she tell you she wants to go to college."

"Well, I thought—"

"Lady," Judd interrupted, "you overstepped your bounds. If my daughter wishes to go to college, she will go! Mayhap I'll have to send her to England, Jamaica, or wherever, if she can't go in this country, but she'll go!"

"Mr. Trumbull, I just thought," Sarah Perkins stuttered, "as a day laborer, you, her father..."

"What I do, ma'am, how I take care of my family, is none of your affair."

Judd's voice was slow and measured as if he were explaining facts to a child.

"Doesn't my daughter, Maribeth, here, make good grades, eh?" He twisted his hat in his hands.

"Yes, she does. Excellent, excellent grades. Some of the highest in the class, I'm happy to say."

"Her mother and I are happy to know that." He looked at his wife Emily, who nodded in silent agreement.

"So . . . we do not expect to hear any more talk of domestic service, do we now?" he asked.

Sarah Perkins shook her head, her face beet-red from the man's chastisement.

"Remember, please teach our child, but make no decisions. Don't meddle in this family's business. Got no more to say. Thank you for de time."

He turned to kiss his daughter on the cheek.

"Have a good day, child. Study hard and do us proud. Come, my dear." He gave his arm to his wife, who also kissed Maribeth good-bye.

"Good day, miss," he said, and they left.

Maribeth went to her assigned seat and sat down. She thought, *What will Miss Perkins do now? Will she punish me for telling my parents what she said?* She busied herself with her books.

Finally, her teacher spoke. Her tone of voice was matter-of-fact and cold.

"Your parents have made it quite clear what they want for you, Maribeth," she said. "Hope you won't be a disappointment to them."

"No, ma'am," Maribeth said. She stared out of

the classroom window and waited for the bell that would start the school day. As her classmates tumbled in noisily, she wondered about her future.

Many times during her high school and college years, Maribeth thought of that day as the turning point in her life. She realized what she owed her parents and she determined to make them proud of her. She would become a teacher. She graduated at the top of her class in high school, but was denied being named valedictorian because the school authorities said she had too many school absences, four; whereas the white classmate second to her had a perfect attendance, so she was chosen for the honor.

Maribeth was discouraged again when she failed to be accepted by the local colleges. It was not her grade but her color that caused her nonacceptance. By now Maribeth had learned that prejudice came in many forms, but she knew she would always recognize it in whatever subtle shapes and nuances it appeared.

"Like I told that teacher woman," her father reminded her, "you're going to college."

She went south to a small teachers' college. She was happy there for two years, studying to be a high school teacher. She planned to teach English and biology, her favorite subjects.

It was the war in Europe that changed so many lives, Maribeth's one of them. During that time, she was reluctant to be so far from her parents, so she returned home. Because of the wartime shortage of nurses, she entered nursing school. She became a skilled professional, recognized as such by other nurses and physicians. She loved nursing, but in the back of her mind was the unfulfilled goal of teaching. As soon as she received her degree she planned to seek a teaching position.

She wondered, sometimes, if she was motivated by the need to prove Miss Perkins wrong. She preferred to believe it was because she never wanted to let her parents down. She knew that was, by far, the more satisfying reason. However, always somewhere deep in her mind was the rankling memory of Miss Perkins's assumption that because *she* was white *she* was somehow entitled, had the authority, to make decisions for Maribeth, who was colored. Maribeth always remembered how inferior she felt. She also remembered how valuable she had felt when her parents faced that white teacher. *I can do anything I set my mind to do. Don't tell me I can't. Not ever!* It was her personal motto and she lived by it. It wasn't that she minded being worried over, but she wanted to make her own decisions and either fail or succeed because of them.

When Maribeth and Ben arrived at the house that Sunday, Maribeth's mother told them dinner was almost ready. But her father and Ben decided to check over the old car first.

"Like to look under the hood, check the oil and water whenever I get the chance," her father advised Ben.

"I agree with that, sir. Was telling your daughter on the way over how important it was to take care of her car."

"Well, son, you know how women are with mechanical things."

"Yes, sir, I know," Ben agreed.

"Table's all set, Mama. Shall I call them in for dinner?"

"May as well, Maribeth. By the time they wash up,

everything will be on the table. Hope your friend likes curried goat."

"Have to be something mighty wrong with the man if he doesn't," Maribeth answered. "But from what I know of him, he does like to eat. Curried goat and rice should satisfy any man's appetite."

"At any rate, if he doesn't care for it I have some fried chicken that he might like."

"Gosh, Mama, don't spoil him! So far Ben is just a good friend. Don't go pairing me up, not yet. Got to get my degree, maybe get an administrative job in nursing, and make some money. And I've really set my heart on getting a teaching position at one of the nursing schools here in Boston, maybe Boston University, in their degree program."

Her mother stopped filling a service dish with hot steaming rice to look directly at her daughter.

"Maribeth, child, I'm the last person to deny you your ambitions, but I want you to know there is nothing more wonderful or more natural than sharing your life with someone you love, who truly loves you in return. Nothing wrong with ambition and a good career, but there's *nothing* that takes the place of a love of a good man. You hear what I'm sayin'?"

She answered her mother, "I hear you, Mama." She thought, *I'm still determined to follow my own path, Mama. Much as I love you and Daddy, got to go down my own road.*

And knowing that her need for independence was increasing, she found a one-bedroom apartment that she could afford. She explained to her mother, "Mama, I know you think I should stay at home, but I do want my own place. . . ."

"Your father thinks you just want to get away from us old fogies," her mother said.

"You know that's not true. Anyway, if I *do* want to have my own place, it's all your fault, both yours and Dad's."

"Child, what you talkin' 'bout, my fault?"

Maribeth grinned, put her arms around her mother. "Emily DeVries Trumbull! Have you ever seen two more independent people than you and Dad? Don't you know 'the apple doesn't fall too far from the tree'?"

"Oh, you! Get out of here!" her mother said.

She slapped Maribeth in the direction of her shoulder as her daughter, laughing, slipped out of her grasp.

But she did continue to date Ben. Some nights he'd bring Chinese food to her apartment.

"Told me you liked fried scallops and shrimp-fried rice," he said.

"I do, Ben, and I see you brought fried chicken wings, my favorite," Maribeth told him.

"Always aim to please, you know."

"Want some coffee?"

"Sure do. Didn't get much sleep today. Working nights is the pits. Didn't sleep well today at all."

"You got to get used to it, Ben, my love. At least you get days off." The police worked four days on, two days off, which changed as the weeks went by. "Like I said," she told him, "I've been with this coronary patient for almost ten days."

"I'm off this weekend. Think you could take the weekend off? We could do something special, maybe. I've saved up a couple of gas ration books."

Maribeth handed him a mug of hot coffee,

sipped from her own cup, and slowly shook her head.

"Can't tell yet, Ben. Really depends on my patient. You know what they say about coronaries—the first three hours after a coronary attack are most critical; then if the patient makes that, it's the next three days. If he gets past that, it's the next ten days before you can say he might make it. So far, my patient has made the ten days. Maybe he won't need me much longer and can go on floor care."

"When will you know? I'm trying to get tickets for Saturday night at Punn's Pub, on the turnpike."

"I'd sure like to hear some good jazz," Maribeth said. "I hear they have real good music there."

"I know I'm ready for some relaxin'," Ben agreed. "We both need a change of pace. I'm over in Charlestown tonight," he told her, "so I'd better get going."

He picked up his tunic jacket, kissed Maribeth quickly on the cheek.

"Don't work too hard, Ben. Keep your powder dry and watch your back!" she advised.

"You too, kid. I know how tough nursing can be sometimes. Don't work too hard, Maribeth. Give me a holler if you need me. Night." And he was gone.

After Ben left, Maribeth cleaned up from their meal, then changed into her uniform and white shoes and stockings. She braided her long red-auburn hair and wound it coronet-style around her head. She was thinking about Ben and how comfortable she felt around him. It seemed as if she had known him for a long time. Her folks, too, were comfortable with him, calling him "son" already. Yes, it would be nice to go to a nightclub. She had been "in the books" with several papers to pass in each week. She did need a breather.

A few more months and she'd have her degree. Would things get serious between them when she graduated?

She picked up her belongings, purse, hat box, and red sweater, grabbed her keys off her dresser, and went out into the cool summer evening.

Maybe . . . when the war is over . . .

Two

Maribeth Trumbull was not the only person at Zion Memorial Hospital who wanted to be on time for appointments. For her it was a matter of pride, for Peter Logan, M.D., it was the need for security, to safeguard; in other words, to make certain all bases were covered. His mother said it best, "Peter never liked surprises. Could never give him a surprise birthday party! He wouldn't stand for it. Go off to his room, never come out. So I stopped tryin'."

He had been granted his requested slot, a two-year internship at the highly ranked Zion Memorial Hospital. He stood in front of the building looking up at the elegant white-faced stone building. Decorative arched windows on each floor formed a classical facade. Five floors soared majestically over glass and metal double doors. Peter thought it looked more like a hotel than a hospital.

Peter Logan's involvement with hotels was limited to one summer, his junior year in high school when he worked as a bellhop at a Boston hotel. It was his muscular, well-built frame that people noticed, along with his orange-red hair. He would never fit the stereotypical picture of an introspective bookish doctor; rather, one of an athlete. With

Peter's six feet-plus, his dad had insisted he had the makings of a championship boxer.

"But, Da, I *know* I can beat any man that gets in the ring with me. I *know* that, but that's not what I want. I want to be a doctor, to heal people, if I can, not break up their bodies."

It was his last year at Boston College. Being on the boxing team was enough. Oh, he loved boxing; one man against the other, it seemed the epitome of masculinity, the sum and substance of male courage, but in the end, what was left? One man's triumph over another man's defeat. Not rewarding enough for him. So here he was, at last, on the threshold of his dream.

He walked purposefully up the smooth granite staircase that led him into an imposing lobby. It did look like a hotel lobby; all that was missing was a uniformed concierge. A large, magnificent chandelier hung from the ceiling over a huge, round mahogany table in the center of the grand rotunda. A decorative vase with a large bouquet of fresh flowers rested on it. Pink calendula, purple asters, blue and white phlox, and other light summer flowers that looked as if they had graced an English garden gave the hospital lobby a desirable feeling of peace and goodwill.

The floor was shiny black marble with wedges of white marble radiating from the center. Peter saw a waist-high counter to the left in the lobby manned by a middle-aged woman. When Peter approached, she glanced up with a look that made him feel as if he were intruding upon someone with more important things than to deal with him. Her white uniform and stiffly starched cap on her head fairly crackled with authority.

MEANT TO BE

She repeated Peter's inquiry. "Pharmacy?"

"Please, ma'am," Peter said quietly, as if he were in the Holy of Holies.

"Basement floor. The stairs are down the corridor to the right," she said. "Pharmacy is at the end of the corridor."

Peter thanked her and moved away quickly. The woman's attitude seemed to indicate he'd be wise to do so.

As he walked away he realized that he had come a long way from a streetwise Irish kid. Indeed . . . a long way from his young days as boxing star of the Boston Police Athletic Association. When the Irish powers at City Hall noticed that the fiery red-haired lad from Mission Hill had made a name for himself when he was offered a scholarship to finish high school at Boston College High; then it was over to Boston College. His father, deprived of his dreams of a boxing champion in the family, changed his dream to having young Pete becoming a "three-eagle," a graduate of Boston College High School, Boston College, and Boston College Law School.

"'Tis a grand lawyer you'd be, son. I know it. You've got the smarts to do it," he said.

Peter's mother had other ideas. She wanted Peter to become a priest.

"There's no finer callin' for any man," she told him. Peter had his own ideas, and when he told them what was in his heart, both parents conceded.

"Ma, Da," he said as gently as he could, "I know you mean well. I love you both, but what I want is medicine. It's the healer's life I'm after. There's too many deaths here from T.B. and alcohol. Too many poor people crowded in these three-deckers. I want to be able to help . . . if I can."

"God bless you, son." His mother held him close. His father shook his son's hand firmly. "It's whatever you want, boyo."

Anxious to get started, Peter could hardly wait. He had decided to scout around and find his way around the famous Zion Memorial. He considered himself lucky to be spending the next two years of his life there. He considered himself an observer-visitor. If anyone questioned him, he could explain that soon, July first, only a few days from now, he would be an intern rotating on the medical service.

So he had dressed as he thought most drug salesmen did: black suit, white shirt, striped tie. He carried a briefcase.

Zion Memorial, a private facility, contained over five hundred beds. Several buildings were connected by tunnels and overhead walkways. With patient care in mind, and to make directions simple for staff and visitors, the hospital had several painted stripes on the floor to lead the visitor or patient to his destination more easily. Peter found the door to the stairwell leading to the lower floor. A map beside the stairwell indicated that the green stripe led to outpatient, the red stripe to emergency and admissions, and the yellow to the various inpatient buildings.

In the basement he found not only the pharmacy department, but various laboratories and the X-ray department. It was a busy work area. White-coated workers milled about. Weary patients in wheelchairs, dressed in hospital garb, covered with blankets, sheets, or robes, were being shuffled in and out of different departments. No one approached him. Peter thought perhaps it was because he acted as if he belonged.

The second time he went to Zion Memorial was two days later. This time he wore a white clinic jacket, a name tag that identified him as Peter Logan, M.D., and he had his stethoscope, a gift from his mother, in his pocket.

Rayna Genrose, his longtime girlfriend from high school, had given him the blue and gold name tag.

"This is for you. I want to be the first person to call you Dr. Logan," she said when she kissed him right after his graduation from medical school. The night before they had spent the night together, knowing that when Peter's parents and extended family arrived they would have little time together. Both knew they were reaching a different stage in their relationship.

"As soon as my internship is over," Peter promised Rayna.

"I'll be waiting," Rayna told him.

This day Peter made his way to a medical unit. It was noon, a busy time for the unit. Patients were being passed food trays, others were still returning from various departments. The main corridor was alive with gurneys, wheelchairs, and even some ambulatory patients who pushed intravenous poles that they were attached to, as they tentatively tried out their wobbly legs. Peter dodged the traffic and walked from one end of the unit to the other. *Soon,* he exulted inwardly, *I'll be working on this very floor, caring for patients, making diagnoses, writing orders for patient care.* He could hardly wait.

Unexpectedly, as he passed a patient's room, the wide door opened and a nurse grabbed him by the arm.

"In here, quick! Cardiac arrest! Code blue!" she shouted in the direction of the nurses' station. She propelled Peter to the patient's bedside. She shoved a small metal box into his hands.

"Here's the cardiac kit! What do you want? Coramine? Caffeine? An amp of epinephrine?" She shoved a syringe with a long needle attached to it at him.

The nurse had drawn up the heart stimulant. Peter looked at the syringe and long needle the nurse had thrust into his hand. He knew he was supposed to inject the medication directly into the heart muscle. Could he do it? *Should* he do it? A man's life was at stake.

He looked at the patient and made a quick assessment. The stricken patient was a white male, probably forty-five years old, he estimated. His skin was bluish gray, which meant he was being oxygen deprived due to his failing heart. His breathing was rapid and shallow. Pale beads of sweat glistened on his pale chest, and the clammy moisture matted his dark hair to his forehead.

"Oxygen increase to seven liters!" Peter snapped. He moved closer to check the man's pulse. The nurse was taking a blood pressure reading.

"Sixty over forty," she told Peter.

Beneath Peter's probing fingers the man's pulse was weak and thready. He had to act. He reached for the intracardiac syringe that he had momentarily laid on the bedside table. He breathed a prayer. *First do no harm* came into his mind from the Hippocratic oath he had sworn to only a week ago. He remembered, too, that Coramine was a preparation to be used in the case of failing heart muscle. He pushed the pajama top to the side, exposing the bare chest. Using the xyphoid bone of the chest as a marker, he placed the fingers of his left hand on the chest to find the tip of the heart. When he found what he thought was the correct spot, he cleaned the skin with the antiseptic sponge the nurse handed him and plunged the four-inch thin needle into the patient's chest. He had been in the room for only one minute.

"Good work," the nurse said, "Dr. . . ."

"Logan. Dr. Peter Logan. I'm to be assigned to this unit tomorrow."

The nurse continued to check the patient. Peter noticed the man's blue pallor had faded somewhat and the color was returning to his face.

"How's the bp now?" he asked.

"Better. One hundred over sixty," she said.

"Pulse is stronger, too, but you'd better let his doctor know about this episode."

"I certainly will, Dr. Logan. I certainly will."

Dr. Peter Logan left the room feeling ten feet tall. He had defeated the Grim Reaper—this time.

Three

It had been a difficult day for Maribeth. Her usual daytime sleep pattern was to get into bed as soon as possible after coming home to her second-floor apartment. Her landlady, Mrs. Edson, a widow in her seventies, was very quiet. Maribeth scarcely knew she was around. So if she could get into bed by eight in the morning, her deepest sleep came immediately. If she was fortunate, she'd remain asleep until eleven or twelve, possibly one. Somehow, it seemed that then the telephone calls would begin. For Maribeth, the worst indignity in the world was to have a salesman telephone to try to interest her in a water-purification system, when that was the last thing she needed. She usually managed to mumble, "No, thanks" and bang the receiver down on the caller, relieving some of her frustration.

She couldn't take the receiver off the hook because the telephone was her lifeline, her source of employment. The Central Directory Agency for Private-Duty Nurses might call. Anything could happen. She might be relieved from her present case, a patient could have died during the day (she seemed to be assigned the most gravely ill patients), or she could have been reassigned to a different patient, or because of the war and shortage of nurses she could be asked to "double up," take an additional patient.

It had been one of those days, a difficult sleep day. She'd fallen asleep the minute her head hit the pillow, but had been awakened by ten. The harsh, scraping, clanking sound of the oil truck's steel nozzle being thrust into the opening of the service tank in the cellar, the gurgling rumble of the oil being pumped into it, the outside door of the hall vestibule slammed shut after the delivery man shoved the bill into the metal mail slot—all intruded into her sleep deprived consciousness like a demon nightmare. Her half sleep was further assaulted by the insistent shrill of a belligerent police siren. Maribeth fumbled sleepily for her watch under her pillow. Only ten-thirty. She punched her pillow in desperate frustration to return to her much-needed sleep. But by now, she was wide awake.

She showered, dressed; brown slacks and a red shirt, Harvard crimson with *Harvard* in bold white letters across the front. Maribeth had taken a summer course at the Harvard School of Public Health and she felt entitled to wear her Harvard sweatshirt. It was at Harvard, with its multiethnic student population, that she was most frequently questioned about her race.

"Are you colored?" some students would ask without preface. Or sometimes she would be asked, "Are you Arabic, Spanish, Italian, from the islands somewhere?"

"Uh-uh. I'm an American Negro," Maribeth would explain patiently. Or if she felt especially put upon, would shrug her shoulders to say, "I am what I am, just me, Maribeth Trumbull, Judd and Emily Trumbull's daughter." She didn't think it was necessary to tell them that her grandmother on her father's side was Lucy Wong. Her father was born in Jamaica to a Chinese mother and a Jamaican father. Judd Trumbull had immigrated to Cambridge, Massachusetts, looking to improve his life.

Maribeth's mother was from New Orleans. It was from Emily Trumbull and Lucy Wong that Maribeth inherited her exotic attractiveness. From her father she received her lithe figure with slender, supple musculature. Her creamy tan coloring, slightly oval dark eyes, and long, silky reddish brown hair confused people and left them wondering. When dressed in her crisp white uniform, her white organdy cap on top of her coiled bun, Maribeth's slender, tall presence made people aware that she was a dedicated professional. Her calm manner exuded confidence and capability.

Driving to work that night, Maribeth wondered what kind of patient she would be assigned. It seemed to her that most of her cases recently had been middle-aged male executives suffering from coronary heart disease or a myocardial infarction, and in either situation she had to be most vigilant the moment she stepped into the patient's room. She knew she had to fight tooth and nail to save the patient's life. She geared herself for the inevitable battle.

Her old Chevy coughed and spat, sputtered spasmodically through the dark streets of Roxbury, through the park, to the wide boulevard where some of Boston's most renowned hospitals were located. She thought of her father's worry. Like Ben, her father had warned her about working the night shift.

"This damn war is swallerin' up every bit of steel

n' iron there is," he told her one night when she made one of her infrequent stops to have supper with her parents.

"You got to be careful drivin' round at night. Car break down, only place you kin git spare parts is mebbe a salvage yard, junkyard, and even then parts scarce as hen's teeth."

"I know, Dad," Maribeth said. "I drive very carefully."

"It ain't that so much. It's that it's hard to keep an old heap runnin'. You know that vehicle of yours has got near a hundred thousand miles on her. Hard to keep an old car like that shipshape. Could be you should work days so you could take the bus."

"But, Dad, then I wouldn't be able to stay in school."

"I know, daughter, an' I'm proud of you for wantin' your college degree. But you got to be practical, too. Anyway, if the old car gives you trouble, let me know, we'll try to keep her runnin' long's we can."

"Dad, thanks, but I'm careful, and I keep gas and oil in the car, check it often."

"Good. Don't want anything to happen to you."

"Oh, Dad, give me some credit! Every night, you know, I make life-and-death decisions in my patient care."

"That's all right, Maribeth, but you're the only child your mother and I have, and whether you know it or not, it's our business to worry about you."

"Yes, Dad," Maribeth said dutifully. But she was glad they were not aware of some of the life-threatening situations their daughter had to face.

Four

Roberta Overton, another private-duty nurse, whispered from the door. She beckoned to Maribeth, who sat knitting beside her sleeping patient's bedside.

"Coffee. Come on down to the kitchen," she whispered.

Her patient, Ned Prescott, was the fifty-five-year-old owner of Prescott Fashions, high-style women's clothing. There was one store in Harvard Square, another on Newbury Street, and a third one on Cape Cod at Osterville. His customers were among the wealthiest in Boston and on the cape.

When the realization of how close he had come to dying finally registered with the high-powered executive, he became as fragile as a child. His fear and dread showed in his pale, worried face.

"Please," he begged Maribeth, "miss, don't leave me. Stay by me, please."

He needed constant reassurance the first week after his coronary heart attack.

Maribeth tried to ease his anxiety. She knew that patients who had had heart attacks often exhibited tense anxiety.

"I'll be here, Mr. Prescott, always close by. Don't worry." Maribeth had a red cardigan sweater that she had knitted. She knit many nights as she kept watch of her acutely ill patients.

"Look," she assured him, "see, here's my red sweater on the chair. If you wake up and see it on the chair there, you know I'm nearby. There's times when I do have to leave the room to check the doctor's order book, to get your medication, things like that. But I'm always close, and you have the signal cord right here"—she showed him—"pinned to your pillow. If I'm at the nurses' desk and you call, I'll be right with you. You're doing fine, sir. Don't worry."

Lines of worry and anxiety still creased Ned Prescott's face as he whispered tentatively, "You really think so?"

"Oh, I do, and so does Dr. Sandifer."

"You're a doll, miss, and when this is over, come to my store in Harvard Square. You should have a nice outfit for yourself. I wouldn't charge you much, don't worry . . . a nice designer suit, maybe . . ."

"Thanks, Mr. Prescott. Now no more talking. You must sleep. Doctor's orders."

Maribeth knew she'd never go to one of Mr. Prescott's upscale shops. Even at the lowest wholesale prices she could never afford the elegant clothing he sold. And with her lifestyle, school during the day, sometimes, and work at night, and the ever-present war in Europe and Japan, where would she go to wear a designer outfit?

A few minutes later, her patient settled and safely asleep, Maribeth joined Roberta in the ward unit's kitchen for coffee. Madeline Kauff, the nursing supervisor, was there as well.

"Well, Maribeth, our finder of dead bodies," she

teased, "I have a message for you from the hospital director's office."

"For me? For what?" Maribeth asked. She felt her face flush and stinging pricks of perspiration needle under her arms and her neck.

"You discovered the body, m'dear."

"But that's all I did. Don't know anything else. Do they know who he is, where he came from?"

"Not sure," the nursing supervisor answered, all levity erased from her voice, "but I gather it's a medical-legal case, and the police want to ask a few questions. Anyway, here's the message." She handed Maribeth a slip of paper that read *Maribeth Trumbull, R.N., Hospital Director's office, 8:00 A.M.*

Maribeth admired Madeline Kauff and had always worked well with the newly married young Jewish nurse. Prepared for her supervisory position with a master's degree from Boston University, she was practical and levelheaded and . . . sincere. Maribeth had found, working with Madeline Kauff, that if she couldn't answer a nursing question, she would immediately say so, but she would always try to find an answer. Maribeth trusted her. She was a nurse's nurse, meaning she was on the side of nursing.

Maribeth took comfort in the supervisor's matter-of-fact attitude. Still she wondered, *Am I being paranoid, would any other nurse be questioned by the police for something as innocent as finding a dead body? Or is it me, because I'm colored? I should know something? Don't even know who the man is. Wonder if I should talk to Ben about this. Should I have a lawyer when the police question me? I know how police can be, sometimes. . . .*

Ben's tour of duty ended at eight in the morning

MEANT TO BE

but he could be delayed by reports to fill out, especially if there had been incidents, arrests during the night. She thought she'd try to call him to see if he could help her out of this dilemma. She hoped she was ready for his inevitable fussing, "You're always getting involved in *something*, Maribeth!" He'd be exasperated, she knew. But what could she do? She had discovered a dead body on the doorstep of one of Boston's most prestigious hospitals.

Maribeth gave a quick report the next morning to Elizabeth Clair, R.N. Thank God Clair always came in early. She wanted to have time for a full report on the patients' conditions before she took over.

"Guess you heard all the excitement that happened last night," Maribeth told her.

"God, yes," Elizabeth Clair said. "It's all over the office. What happened?"

Elizabeth was a middle-aged nurse who had spent most of her professional life working at Zion Memorial. She was on the plump side, but everyone knew, doctors and nurses alike, that in a medical crisis no one could move faster or work more efficiently than Elizabeth Clair, R.N.

"Let me give you my report on Mr. Prescott first," Maribeth told her as they moved from the sleeping patient's bedside to a conference room nearby. Maribeth opened her patient's chart.

"He had a good night, best so far, actually," she told the day nurse. "Blood pressure has stabilized around one-fifty over eighty-eight. His pulse is good, running between seventy-six and eighty. Respirations are normal. He's voiding okay, and his intake is good. Last night was one of his best."

"Dr. Sandifer said yesterday that he was pleased with his condition. He could even be discharged in a day or two. Now, tell me about the dead man!" Elizabeth Clair's eyes widened with interest at the opportunity to hear what Maribeth had to say.

"Clair," Maribeth said (nurses often spoke to each other by their last name), "I was just coming on duty, you know it's real dark with the blackout and all, and I had my flashlight on and ... there he was. I thought it was a pile of rags, and you know how Dr. Rudkin is about clutter and stuff around the hospital."

"I know, he'd have a fit. So I hear the police are going to question you?" The older nurse's excitement was palpable and Maribeth knew she wanted to know more. She rose to her feet and gave Elizabeth Clair the patient's chart.

"Got to get going," she said. "Have a good day. See you in the morning, maybe."

Maribeth freshened up the best she could. She combed and secured her long hair into a neat bun and replaced her nurse's cap to appear in full uniform at the hospital director's office. She made her way down the quiet carpeted hall to the office located on the first floor adjacent to the ornate lobby.

The secretary in the outer office offered Maribeth a chair, saying, "Dr. Rudkin is with the police. Would you like some coffee?"

Maribeth did not need more stimulation, so she declined. "No, thanks, I'm fine."

She looked at the pale blue walls of the secretary's office. Wooden-framed plaques, citations, presentations, and awards that the Harvard-educated Dr. Noel Rudkin had received almost covered the walls. His most prestigious diplomas, honors, and degrees were on the walls of his office, Maribeth surmised.

The furniture was functional but comfortable. The carpet was a soft muted green that relaxed Maribeth somewhat. She took a deep breath, muttered a prayer to herself, and remembered Ben saying long ago when they were talking about giving testimony to police, "Never volunteer information. Answer only what you're asked, nothing more, and never answer a question you're not sure of. Better to say 'I don't know.'"

So, she reflected, she wouldn't say anything about the motor she thought she heard that sounded like a truck, nor the strange odor she noticed . . . not a regular antiseptic odor that one associated with hospitals. It was more of a rank, charred smell, like burned flesh. The unforgettable odor she had first come in contact with when she had cared for a survivor of the Coconut Grove fire, one of Boston's worst fires. It was a smell that any nurse would recognize. Had the dead man been in a fire? she wondered.

When she was finally escorted into Dr. Rudkin's office by his secretary, she found him sitting behind his desk. The police officer, dressed in plainclothes, sat at his left. Both men rose immediately as she came in and the director reached across his desk to shake her hand.

"Come in, Miss Trumbull. Please have a seat." He indicated a chair that had been placed in front of his desk. "This is Officer McKey." He introduced the man, who shook her hand.

"Miss Trumbull," he acknowledged.

"We know that you have been on duty all night, and I, for one, appreciate the time you are giving us to help with this investigation," the director said. "I haven't forgotten what it is like to be up all night." He smiled. "So we'll get right to it. Officer . . . ?"

Maribeth turned slightly in her seat to look at the policeman. He appeared to be about thirty, Ben's age, she thought. He was conservatively dressed: dark trousers, an oxford-type shirt with a striped tie, and a tweed jacket with leather elbow patches.

He cleared his throat before he spoke. His pencil was poised over his notepad, ready for her answers.

"Miss Trumbull." His voice was firm and he spoke with the authority of the Boston Police Department. "What time was it when you found the body?"

Maribeth steeled herself to stay calm although she could feel rivulets of nervous perspiration creep annoyingly down her neck. She took a deep breath and exhaled before she answered.

"About ten-fifty."

"Did you see anyone else around?"

"No."

"And how did you find the victim?"

"He was just lying there. I had my flashlight, it's so dark now with the blackout and all, I thought someone had left a bundle of rags."

"Why did you pay attention to a bundle of rags?" The policeman raised his eyebrows in twin question marks, his pencil poised over his notepad, ready for Maribeth's answer.

"Dr. Rudkin . . ." She looked at the hospital director, who responded with an encouraging smile. "Dr. Rudkin," she continued, "has always stressed that the hospital grounds, the environment should be well kept as a reflection of the hospital itself. I knew that a bundle of rags had no place on the front steps of the hospital. That's why I checked." She noticed a brief nod of agreement from the director.

"I see. Well, thank you very much . . . Miss Trumbull, is it?"

"Yes," Maribeth answered calmly even though her insides were jumpy. "Miss Maribeth Trumbull." Had he forgotten her name that quickly?

She had maintained eye contact throughout the interview. She hoped her manner and her tone of voice covered the nervousness she felt.

With few exceptions, news of the war covered most of the front page of the *Boston Post Dispatch* when Maribeth had a chance to read it before she went to sleep a few mornings later.

BERLIN BOMBED BY 800 US. FLYING FORTRESSES
ALLIED FORCES ENTER ROME

Then there was:

CIRCUS TENT FIRE OF BARNUM AND BAILEY,
RINGLING BROTHERS CIRCUS CLAIMS 167

Maribeth shuddered when she read that item. More burn victims, she thought. *Hope the treatment the doctors learned from treating the Grove victims will help. At least now there are antibiotics available.* But down in the lower right-hand corner she found what she had been searching for.

Police have identified the victim found on the hospital steps as Bernardo D'Asardi, thirty-five, also known as Bernie Hazzard, a local middleweight boxer. His last bout, said to be two nights ago, brought him a defeat. It was a knockout in the ninth round of a ten-round battle by his opponent, Tim Sippowicz, a contender for the New England middleweight championship. Hazzard was said to have been winning the fight before the knockout. Police are investigating.

Maribeth folded the newspaper and dropped it to the floor beside her bed. She knew she'd better get to sleep. She hoped sleep would not be long in coming. It was a rainy, dark morning, and the bleak gray skies made it seem more like night. Perhaps she would have some decent sleep after all . . . if she could get Bernie Hazzard out of her mind. Where *had* the smell of burnt flesh come from? Where was the truck whose motor she heard? Why had the police even questioned her? She tried to push the unanswered questions from her mind as she fought with her busy mind for sleep.

That night, when Maribeth arrived at her patient's room, the evening nurse had tried to prepare Mr. Prescott for a good night's sleep. But Mr. Prescott was anxious to see Maribeth and tell her himself that he was going home the next day.

"You can see now," the other nurse told Maribeth, "why I did not sedate him earlier. You may need that 'prn' to settle him down, you can see he's so 'up,'" she told Maribeth. A "prn" was medication the doctor had ordered to be used "as necessary," but Maribeth knew the medication was for one time only. Most sedatives were.

"Home tomorrow, Miss Trumbull! Isn't that

great news?" The patient's face beamed with anticipation.

"It's wonderful news, Mr. Prescott." Maribeth purposefully kept her voice low and calm. "I'm glad for you. But you'd better settle down for a good night's rest. I'm going to check your vital signs and give you something to help you sleep."

Ned Prescott was excited. His blood pressure was stable, but his pulse rate was a little high and he was restless, kept moving around in his bed. Maribeth frowned. She realized she would have to quiet her patient somehow. Perhaps she'd have to use the sedative order soon if Mr. Prescott didn't get to sleep. She knew the restlessness and excitement were not good, especially in a cardiac patient.

She lowered the lights in the room. Left only a small lamp on near the chair she usually occupied. She turned the reflector shade until there was only a small soft glow. Murmuring softly in a low, quiet tone of voice she encouraged her patient to try to sleep. She stroked his back with hospital lotion, tightened his sheets, offered him a cool drink, and arranged pillows for his comfort.

"Have a good night, Mr. Prescott," she encouraged him.

"Um-m-m, I'll try. Miss Trumbull?"

"Yes, what is it?"

He was still hyperactive. She could hear it in his voice.

"Call my wife, please."

"It's late, sir."

"What, eleven-thirty? She never goes to bed until after twelve. Call her," he insisted, half turned from his side position. "Tell her I'm coming home, be discharged at eleven. Tell her I've arranged for

Thomas, my manager from the Harvard Square store, to bring me home. She should not bother herself to come for me. You'll tell her that?"

"I will. I'll do it now. Promise you'll try to rest." She left to make the call, closing the door softly behind her.

"Yes, Mrs. Prescott? This is Miss Trumbull, your husband's night nurse. No, he's doing well, about to fall asleep—"

Mr. Prescott's wife interrupted.

"Dr. Sandifer called today already. My husband's being discharged?"

"That's correct, Mrs. Prescott, around eleven or so, but he wanted me to tell you to sit tight and wait for him to get home."

"Oh, I'll be waiting, Miss Trumbull, tell him that! And . . . thanks for taking such good care of my husband."

"My pleasure, ma'am. Good night. Got to get back to my patient. Good night now, and good luck."

As Maribeth left the bank of public phones located in the north corridor adjacent to the private room sector (most physicians felt that telephones were too stressful to be allowed in a cardiac patient's room) she thought, *If my patient does go home today, I will be free this weekend after all. I can spend time with Ben.* She wasn't yet sure of their relationship, or where it was headed, but she did enjoy being with him. There weren't that many able-bodied young men around, especially colored men; all were serving overseas. She was lucky to have a friend like Ben and she knew it.

MEANT TO BE

She pushed open the door to her patient's room and he turned his head to smile expectantly at her.

"What did my wife say?" His face was bright with joyful anticipation.

"She says she's going to sit tight, can't wait to see you."

"I can't wait either," he said. "'Sit tight'," he said. "That's our favorite—"

Suddenly, Ned Prescott grabbed at his chest.

"What is the matter, Mr. Prescott? What's wrong?"

"Can't breathe," he gasped. "Pain, oh . . ."

At once Maribeth heard the moist gurgles and choking sounds that meant to her that her patient was suddenly in acute distress. His face was gray-white and bathed in clammy sweat. *Oh God! He's going into cardiac arrest!*

She steeled herself to be calm, to remember the procedures she must do in such a grave emergency. Her patient's life was at stake.

She sprang into action, pulled the bell cord, yelled into the intercom on the panel above the patient's head, "Code blue, stat! Room twenty-seven! Code blue, stat!"

She turned on the suction machine, shoved a rubber catheter into the man's mouth and throat to clear his airway, quickly placed the oxygen mask over his nose and mouth, and increased the oxygen flow. She heard the running footsteps of the cardiac team and they came in as she was trying to get a read on the patient's blood pressure.

Dr. Peter Logan questioned, "What is it?"

"Ninety over forty, pulse is weak and thready," Maribeth told him.

"Cut-down kit!" Dr. Logan snapped to a nurse on the team. "And give me one amp of the vasodilator." To another nurse he said, "Draw blood for blood gasses," and to Maribeth, "I want five percent DW set up! Stat!"

Peter Logan checked the patient's heartbeat with his stethoscope, muttered something, and shook his head.

It seemed as if everyone in the room was doing something to help the patient in his battle. Maribeth maintained her position, monitoring and checking her patient's vital signs. She looked at the red-haired intern, his face flushed almost beet-red by his intense anxiety as he tried to save Ned Prescott's life.

Maribeth's fingers moved frantically from her patient's wrist to his jawline to the carotid artery in his neck to the temporal artery in his forehead as she tried to find a palpable pulse.

Dr. Logan had thrown back the covers at the foot of the bed to expose the patient's foot. He quickly cleaned an area near the patient's ankle, inserted a large needle into the vein, and attached an intravenous solution. That done, he returned again to listen to the patient's heartbeat with his stethoscope. Then Maribeth saw him administer a sharp blow to the patient's chest with his balled-up fist.

"Come on, damn it!" he shouted. "Don't give up!"

Maribeth thought she had never seen such a large fist. This doctor looked more like a football player, thick neck and shoulders, wire-coiled red hair, and red-faced in his frantic attempt to revive the patient. He looked like an angry young man, upset at fighting a losing battle. The futile thumps he continued to strike on the man's chest could be heard all over the room. He was trying to jump-start the heart. Sometimes such action was effective.

Maribeth caught Peter's eyes and shook her head. She could not feel a pulse and there was only a faint blood pressure reading. Her patient gave a long sigh and then there was a massive silence in the room.

Angrily, Peter Logan tore the stethoscope from his neck and shoved it into his jacket pocket.

"Who's his doctor?" he demanded.

"Dr. Sandifer, chief of staff," Maribeth said.

"Damn, better call him." He looked at the patient. Ned Prescott's eyes stared sightlessly at the ceiling. Peter Logan looked at the wall clock. "I'm pronouncing him dead at one-oh-five," he said. "Thanks, everyone, for trying."

He stumbled out of the room. This time the Grim Reaper had won.

Maribeth was alone in the room with the dead man. She looked at his pale, flaccid face. Had she done all she could to save him? What more could she have done?

God, be with him, she breathed and turned to open the postmortem kit. *Sometimes nursing can be so hard,* she thought.

Five

Michal Strauss Sandifer, M.D., was a true ZMH product. A graduate of Harvard and Harvard Medical School, he had interned at Zion Memorial, completed his residency there, and had finally received a staff position on completion of his residency. After several years during which his own private practice grew, he was made chief of the hospital's medical staff. In addition he was a professor of cardiac medicine at Harvard and had been involved in research into the changes in the heart's normal sinus rhythms during cardiac distress and was looking into a method for using an outside electrical power source to stimulate and pace the heart if the heart's own pacemaker was compromised. That night he had already talked to the young intern, Peter Logan, when he came into the hospital. Now he questioned Maribeth.

"What happened?" he asked gently. This young colored nurse had been highly recommended, but he wanted her own account of the incident.

"Dr. Sandifer, the patient was restless when I came on duty. Excited about being discharged, he asked me to call his wife. When I left him, his vital signs were stable. See here, sir"—she indicated her reference on the patient's chart—"I've documented all the vital signs. His blood pressure at that time was one hundred twenty-eight over sixty-eight. His respirations were regular at eighteen and his pulse was a little high, ninety-two, but it's been like that all along."

"I know," the doctor agreed. "I'll have to get a look at his heart when we do a postmortem," he murmured, almost to himself "In the meantime, Miss Trumbull, Mrs. Prescott is on her way. She wants to see him. Please do what you can to make it easy for her."

Maribeth said she would do her best.

Miriam Prescott was tall, blond, and composed. She was accompanied by a pair of middle-aged men wearing black suits and black Homburg hats. Morticians, Maribeth guessed. The Prescotts were childless.

Although it was two in the morning, Mrs. Prescott looked as if she had just awakened from a refreshing sleep. Her sleek blond hair was worn in an elaborate French twist, her makeup defined her eyes, cheeks, and mouth. She wore an exquisitely cut black linen suit, and a long white cashmere coat was slung over her shoulders against the night air. Her black pumps and fashionable black leather shoulder bag that hung by a gold chain completed her outfit. Her jewelry was a pair of pearl earrings and a strand of pearls around her neck.

Maribeth had removed all the medical paraphernalia that had surrounded the patient from his bedside. She had combed his hair, washed his face, and he did appear to be asleep. In her uniform pocket Maribeth had two ampoules of smelling salts in case the new widow should need them.

"I'm very sorry, Mrs. Prescott," Maribeth murmured as the group approached the bedside.

"Thank you," the woman said in a quiet voice. She leaned over to kiss her husband, turned to the black-suited men, and said cryptically, "Tonight, I *know* where Ned is." Without breaking stride, she turned and left the room, trailing a lingering scent of expensive perfume.

Maribeth remembered the rumors she had heard when she first signed on to the case. It seemed that Ned Prescott had a questionable reputation. "He never met a beautiful woman he couldn't love." The story Maribeth heard was that he had been involved with several other women during his marriage. However, Miriam Prescott accepted her husband's weakness, had remained Mrs. Ned Prescott. And, as she had said, never again would she have to wonder where he was or with whom.

Maribeth sighed as the door closed behind the night visitors, and she prepared to take her patient to the morgue. As a private-duty nurse she had the responsibility to "close up" the patient's chart and remove the dead body to the morgue after she had completed preparing the body.

She put in a page for Fred Stiles, the night orderly, who came up to room 27 with a stretcher. He also had the keys to the morgue room in the basement.

Fred Stiles had been night orderly at ZMH for years. Close to retirement age, his hair thick and white, his eyes tired but nonetheless unemotional to the many unfortunate human situations he handled daily, he was always a willing assistant to the nurses and patients of Zion Memorial Hospital.

"Why do elevators to the morgue move so slowly, Fred?" Maribeth asked.

"What's the hurry?" he replied dryly.

"I guess," Maribeth answered. "No need to hurry now. It's over."

Fred helped her lift the body from the stretcher onto the drawer that he pulled from the refrigerated space. Maribeth completed the procedure she was required to do by attaching a name tag to the slot on the door that matched the one on Mr. Prescott's great toe, right foot.

"God be with you, Mr. Prescott," she whispered again as she hurried from the cold room with its glistening rows of shiny refrigerator doors. She glanced at her watch. Two-thirty. She hoped she could finish up, leave the hospital soon, and get home while it was still dark to get some real sleep.

"Say," Fred questioned as he pushed the empty stretcher into the corridor and locked the morgue room door, "aren't you the nurse that found the body the other night?"

Maribeth gave him a dubious smile, nodded, and said, "It was me all right. Wish now I hadn't."

"He's still down here, you know . . . the guy you found. . . ."

"Two days and they haven't posted him yet?"

"Oh, they did the post, but the medical examiner said everything was normal. Now they want to check for poisons. Some kind . . ."

For someone who dealt with trips to the morgue every day and who had witnessed many causes of death, Fred Stiles shuddered, which surprised Maribeth.

Almost in a whisper, Fred answered softly, "Some kind of strange poison, some rare kind."

"Wow."

"I know, miss. Wow. And I heard that they've isolated the body until they know definitely what it is."

Both she and Fred signed the documentation book in the morgue office as required by hospital procedure. Together they walked to the elevator.

"So the preliminary exam showed no cause of death for the man I found?" She thought about the distinctive odor of burned flesh she had noticed, but said nothing.

"From what I heard the scuttlebutt is that everything was normal except for the blow on his jaw, which shouldn't have killed him, and the strange white stuff around his mouth. Hadn't choked to death, they said, so what made him die like that?"

"Beats me."

"Wouldn't surprise me if the police come around with more questions."

"Well, I know I don't have any answers," Maribeth said. "I only had the misfortune to find him, that's all."

"I hear the hospital director's not too happy with all this attention the hospital's getting," Fred volunteered.

Maribeth tried to defend her position. "It's a hospital with people with problems, isn't it? Things happen in a place like this, I guess."

"Right. You're right. God knows I've seen some things."

They had reached the main floor.

"Thanks for your help, Fred."

"No problem. See you around."

"Sure," Maribeth answered as she returned to the private room floor. She thought, this was the second death she'd been involved in in the past two days. Would there be a third? They say death comes in threes.

She yanked the sheets from the empty bed and completed stripping the room. Mr. Prescott's belongings were bagged and tagged. She opened the window to air the room, emptied the wastebasket. Housekeeping would clean the room in the morning, prepare it for the next patient. Maribeth gathered her handbag and sweater. As she left the room she knew now she could spend the weekend with Ben.

Could she use that time to convince him to help her investigate this murder . . . if that's what it was? She had a nagging need to know what really happened to Bernie Hazzard.

But she also had a feeling that Ben Daniels would not be interested, nor would he want her to become involved in what clearly could be defined as police work. If she insisted on investigating the incident without him, what would this mean to their relationship? She'd try him out on the idea of going to the arena where the boxing match had taken place. Maybe someone there knew something.

They were on their way to the nightspot on the North Shore when Maribeth brought up her idea. Right away Ben let her know he did not approve. "You know, Maribeth, my love, it could be dangerous for you meddlin' in police business. *I* really shouldn't let you get involved. I certainly don't have any right to get involved. I *know* better. I'm not assigned . . . it's not in my district. . . ." He ticked off his reasons.

"I know, I know, Ben, but—"

"I know, too. You're so stubborn. When anyone says you can't, it's like a red flag—"

She protested, "If it's goin' to cause trouble for you, I'll go by myself."

Ben slammed his hand down on the steering wheel. "Said I'd go! Maribeth, stop tryin' to put words in my mouth!" He reached over and squeezed her hand. "My dear, I can be just as hardheaded as you! Any goin' to be done, we'll do it together. You hear, *together!*"

Ben concentrated on negotiating his car around the infamous rotary near Revere before he spoke again. When he did, Maribeth heard unmistakable tension in his voice.

"I forgot to ask you, what are you going down there for, anyway? What do you expect to find?" he asked Maribeth.

Ben honked his horn furiously at a young driver who tried to jump into traffic ahead of him. "Stupid fool," he muttered.

"Ben," she said, hoping to convince him of something she had doubts about, "I just need to know what happened to the man and . . . it's a place to start. After all, he was a boxer and had just been in a boxing match."

"Sometimes, my dear, the *need* to know can get you into more trouble. I know the police know what to do."

"I know, Ben. But somehow the more I know, the better I'll be able to cope with . . . well . . . with whatever. Besides, I'd like to know why a young, apparently healthy boxer dies, practically on a hospital doorway, particularly when he didn't have a heart attack."

"How do you know it wasn't his heart? You're not a doctor."

"I *know* that," she answered testily, "but I'm no

dummy, either. If it was his heart, the autopsy would have shown that straight off."

"Maribeth," Ben apologized, "I didn't say you were a dummy. I just worry that you might bite off more than you can chew, that's all. Besides, like I said, it's a police matter."

"I know, Ben. I know what you mean. I'm not trying to be stubborn or hard to get along with...." She stopped talking as if not sure of what she really wanted to say. She stared silently out of the window.

"What you mean is we've always got to prove ourselves," Ben said softly.

"I guess that's part of it," she conceded. "I keep wondering if the police think I know more than I do, although I don't know why. That officer gave me a funny feeling."

"John McKey? He's usually a pretty fair, straightforward cop."

"I don't know, Ben, there was just something ... the way he questioned me. Like colored people are always into something."

Ben concentrated on his driving. "Well, I don't like your getting mixed up with a police investigation, and I know they won't like it, either."

"I'm just like any other citizen trying to find the truth," Maribeth argued. "But I promise I'll do my best not to embarrass you, Ben."

"Um-m-m ... you be careful whatever you do. Remember, you could be dealing with some tough characters, especially down at the gym."

From Ben's attitude about the matter, Maribeth thought she'd better not tell him too much—he would only worry—such as her plan to visit the late Bernie Hazzard's parents in Concord. They had a roadside stand, sold fruit and vegetables, wouldn't be hard to find. For some reason Maribeth felt compassion for a family she'd never met.

They were both quiet for a while, both with their own thoughts on the dead man. Finally, Ben shook himself, patted the steering wheel, and broke the silence.

"My mom got a letter from Junie yesterday."

"Junior, your brother? Is he okay? How's he doing?" Maribeth asked.

"Fine, from his letter. Course he can't say much. We know he's close to the African front. We'll be glad when this war is over and he comes home."

"I know you will, Ben, especially your mom."

"Yeah, it's hard on her. She worries all the time. She thinks he may even be sent to the Pacific. And that would be hard to take."

Ben looked over at the young woman who sat beside him. She wore a white crepe skirt, a blue jacket decorated with a row of small white buttons, and a red-and-white-striped silk blouse that had a soft tie at the neck. Her red-brown hair was in a sleek pageboy that clung softly to her shoulders. She had never looked lovelier to him. His groin tightened as he realized he was beginning to care very much about her. She was so single-minded, so independent. And . . . he was worried about her quest down the treacherous path she seemed determined to pursue. He drew in a deep breath. He'd have to help her do whatever it was she wanted to do and protect her any way he could.

He stole another glance at Maribeth as she stared thoughtfully out of her car window. He knew that underneath that exciting patriotic-looking outfit was a warm lovely body that he ached to hold. Would that day ever come? Maribeth liked him, he

MEANT TO BE 67

knew that. She wasn't dating anyone else that he knew of, her focus was on her nursing degree and her nursing career—and now on this stupid mystery. He had to admit to himself that he loved and admired her. She was single-minded and goal-oriented, and her self-assurance intrigued him. He'd have to help her—see that nothing untoward happened to her. This was some kind of woman he'd fallen in love with. God help him.

Maribeth took a few days off. As usual, Central Directory called her for another case, this time a brain-injured teenager who had been in a car accident. She declined, saying she was just coming off a long case.

Her car behaved beautifully as she drove along the highway. It seemed to her that the Chevy was glad to be out on the road. It hummed along, giving Maribeth a sense of adventure. What would she find this bright summer day? she wondered as she took the exit sign to Concord.

D'Asardi Farms was easy to find. Maribeth had no idea of what she was going to say or do when she got to the farm. Perhaps play it by ear and do what came naturally to her.

She saw a very colorful vegetable stand on the roadside in front of a well-kept white farmhouse. Maribeth noticed several cars ahead of her that had pulled into the circular drive. Open bins and shelves were filled to overflowing with corn, tomatoes that glistened like jewels, yellow carrots, deep red beets, some with their lush green leaves still attached, as well as earth-brown potatoes. There were green, red, and yellow peppers. Their smooth firm flesh intrigued Maribeth. She moved toward them. Then she saw fresh strawberries and garnet-red raspberries. Maribeth smiled at herself as she realized her mouth was beginning to water. She had an idea. She'd take some fruits and vegetables over to Cambridge to her folks. They would love some farm-fresh produce. She wondered if fresh eggs were for sale as well. Eggs were in short supply because of the war. Her father used to say, "Nothing starts a good day better than a good fresh egg, akee, n' rice. Yeah, man, every real Jamaican knows that!"

She became aware that someone had approached her side. She turned from the strawberry baskets to see a small dark-haired woman who gave her a tentative smile.

"I can help you with something, miss?" The woman's accent was soft, a mellifluent Italian speech pattern.

Almost instinctively Maribeth realized this must be Bernie's mother. Although she smiled, there was a sadness in her eyes that Maribeth recognized as painful sorrow.

"Yes, I'd like some strawberries, two quarts please, and"—she moved over to the vegetables—"a half dozen ears of corn, six tomatoes, and some green and red peppers."

Maribeth knew her mother could cook up a quick gumbo and perhaps make a strawberry shortcake for dessert.

"Do you have fresh eggs?" she asked the woman as the produce was being bagged and weighed.

"Eggs we got. Yes, fresh from the henhouse," the woman sighed. "One dozen large?"

"Yes, please, one dozen large," Maribeth repeated.

MEANT TO BE

"Sal," the woman called out, "from the cooler bring a dozen large eggs."

"Right away, Rini."

The man was heavyset, but not overly fat. His thinning hair was combed carefully to cover a bald spot. He brought the eggs to his wife and Maribeth saw the look of concern he showed her. Maribeth noticed that most of the customers that had preceded her were going to their cars and driving off. She decided to speak about what was on her mind but waited until her bill had been totaled. As she handed over the money she said quietly, "I'm very sorry about the loss of your son." She saw quick tears flood into Rini D'Asardi's eyes and her face blanched quickly.

"I was the nurse who found him," Maribeth added. With a hissing sound, the woman drew in a deep breath.

From the cash register where he was making change, Sal D'Asardi whirled around to face Maribeth. He had overheard what Maribeth had said and saw the pained look in his wife's face. He moved quickly to face Maribeth while holding his wife close with a protective arm around her shoulder. Together they faced Maribeth.

"*You* found my son?"

Maribeth nodded. Then she hesitated. Should she have told them? She swallowed hard, then continued.

"I was going on duty at the hospital . . ."

"You're a nurse? What?"

"I'm a nurse, Mr. D'Asardi. I do private-duty nursing. I'm often at Zion Memorial."

Both Sal and Rini were extremely agitated now as they realized that Maribeth may have been the last person to have seen their child. Their facial movements mirrored their distress.

"Come. Come in the house," Sal implored Maribeth. "You must tell us all you know. Louis!" he called to a young man who was bringing fresh corn to the stand. "Watch the stand for a minute. This nurse found your brother!" He beckoned to Maribeth. "Come in the house," he insisted.

Maribeth noticed the strange look that came over the young man's face when his father ordered him to "watch the stand for a minute." It was obvious that to watch the stand was the last thing the young man wanted to do. He had a sinister look in his eyes, just a fleeting flicker of resentment that was clearly apparent to Maribeth. She shivered as she followed the middle-aged couple into their home. She felt that something was not quite right at this farm despite the glowing appearance of its produce. She had no way of knowing how correct her assumption was.

Louis D'Asardi, the sixteen-year-old son, made a note of Maribeth's presence as he distributed the ears of fresh corn on the roadside stand. He also checked her license plate and memorized the number, 409PT, a Massachusetts plate.

He decided to look into that bit of evidence, find out what he could about the nosy broad. He'd worked too hard to have anyone mess up his plans. He'd overheard her say she was a nurse and had found Bernie. At least Bernie had had the good sense to die on the steps of the hospital, not at home. That would have been hard on the folks, he'd have to admit.

Maribeth put her purchases into her car and followed the anxious couple inside. The house seemed to be a sprawling farmhouse with extended wings from each side of the main house. Maribeth saw what seemed to be a sunroom behind which she glimpsed a beautiful terrace, a relaxing space with lawn chairs and colorful umbrellas. As they entered the main house Maribeth realized with a deep sense of guilt that she had believed she'd see a dark, ornate Italian setting. She was pleasantly surprised to find herself in a light, airy, comfortable living room. A floral couch was placed in front of a black marble, elegantly decorated fireplace. The carpet was a muted beige with pale green accents woven into it. It was a cheerful room. The only concession to the recent grief of the D'Asardi family was a black-draped photograph of Bernie on the sofa table. He had posed in the typical boxer's stance: fists upraised, body poised to attack his opponent.

"Sit, miss, please." Sal D'Asardi offered Maribeth one of the beige leather chairs on either side of the sofa. His wife had disappeared as soon as they had come into the house. Now she returned with a tray. Coffee and anisette cookies were arranged with some of the most elegant, delicate china service that Maribeth had ever seen.

Sal cleared his throat before he spoke. His voice shook as he continued to speak. "You know Bernie was my oldest son. Parents shouldna' have to go through with what we did last week. To bury a firstborn." He shook his head sadly. "Please, you'll have coffee, then tell us, Miss . . ."

"Miss Trumbull. Maribeth Trumbull."

She accepted the coffee Mrs. D'Asardi offered her, declined the cookies with a wave of her hand.

"I'm sorry I've really no more to tell you than

what I already said. It was late at night, almost eleven, it was very dark, the blackout, you know, and I was on my way up the hospital steps when I spotted him on the steps. I thought maybe he had fallen but I could see right away that he was . . . was dead," she said softly.

Mrs. D'Asardi gasped at Maribeth's words and shoved her fist into her mouth to stifle a cry.

Her husband put his arm around her and led her to the sofa where they sat together.

"I wish there had been something I could have done to help him."

"I know, I know," Bernie's father said. "You would have helped if you could. But why did Bernie go to the hospital? He told me he was coming home right after the fight. Went to the market that morning, then said he was going to the gym . . . was going to talk to Roscoe Dunlap, his manager-trainer, rest before the fight, and he'd be home after. Do you know, Miss Trumbull"—his voice lowered as if he didn't want to say the next phrase that came to his lips—"on my son's death certificate it says, 'Death due to poison, toxicology studies inconclusive'? So what does that mean to me, eh?"

"I don't really know, sir."

"To me it means someone poisoned my kid. I want to know who did it and why!"

"I'm sure the police will find all that out, Mr. D'Asardi," Maribeth said. As she rose to leave, she shook hands with Sal D'Asardi, but Bernie's mother grasped Maribeth in a soft hug. "Thank you," she whispered. "Thank you."

Maribeth got in her old Chevy, pulled away from the circular drive. She could see the bereaved couple standing arm in arm in the doorway. She did not see their remaining son standing almost hidden by the opened barn door as he watched her drive away.

Roscoe Dunlap, she thought. At least she had a name to start with when she and Ben went to the gym in the north end of Boston.

She had finally told Ben about her visit to the D'Asardi family. As she expected, Ben was very upset with her.

"As usual, Maribeth, you're getting into something that's way out of your league," he said angrily. "You don't know anything about police work! Nursing, that's your thing. Stick to that and leave policing to the police!"

"Ben, don't lecture me, please! I'm not trying to do police work, or even trying to outsmart the police. But I do want to help that poor family if I can. Besides, the police act as if I know something, which I don't! Not yet, anyway."

Ben sighed deeply.

"What I'm really going to *try* to do is protect you, Maribeth, because I really don't think you know what you're doing."

The place smelled. It smelled of sweat, body odor, liniment, unguents of every description. Maribeth took a deep breath as the noxious odors assailed her nose. There was a noise level that assaulted her ears. In every available spot in the large room half-naked young men were slamming staccato attacks with gloved fists on punching bags. Others were slugging it out on body bags that swung slowly from the gym's smoky ceiling as they were pummeled and pounded by eager young warriors all trying to improve their speed and accuracy. Grunts of pain mingled with bombastic orders barked by trainers as they tried to lead these would-be someday champions to the glory and honor of a championship.

There was a squared-off roped platform in the center of the large room. Maribeth and Ben walked toward it, drawn by the action. Two boxers, dressed in head and body protectors, were sparring. The couple watched, openmouthed. Sweating, grunting as they exchanged blows, the boxers moved around the ring.

A third man, older, yelled at his fighter.

"Use that jab! That's it! Now move, move! What's the matter? Jab! Jab, I said. Do it or back to the goddamn bag! That's right, jab. Now the right. You got two hands, use 'em!"

Engrossed in the action in front of them, neither Ben nor Maribeth saw the small, swarthy-faced man who approached them.

"Somepin' I kin do fer you folks?" he questioned.

Ben whirled around at the sound of the voice, upset because he hadn't been aware that there was anyone nearby.

"We're looking for Roscoe Dunlap."

"You found him."

Six

Roscoe Dunlap, a small wiry man with sinewy muscles, might have been a former welterweight, Ben thought, as the older man hitched up his shoulders as if to do battle. He walked toward the couple with a rolling gait, his face marked with scars and cicatrices that bore evidence of his ring career.

Ben spoke up. "Mr. Dunlap, we're here to ask you about Bernie Hazzard. Understand you were his trainer."

Maribeth noticed a painful expression cross over the trainer's face. He seemed more distressed than ever. He walked over to his cluttered desk and motioned to his visitors to have seats before he sat down.

"Don't know nuthin' 'bout Bernie's dyin'. Nuthin'!"

His voice was low and less agitated as he continued to speak. She was also surprised that even though he had just said he knew "nuthin'," he now seemed to want to talk.

"Bernie was one o' the sweetest kids I ever managed. One o' the best. Smart, listened to ya, tried to do his damnedest every roun'. Every fight wuz special to 'im. Woulda made a great middleweight champ."

"Mr. Dunlap," Maribeth asked, "why did he lose the fight? Didn't the papers say he was ahead?"

Roscoe swept a quick gesture across his eyes as if to clear away the unshed tears. He focused his gaze directly at Maribeth and answered her question. His concern was quite evident in his quick response.

"Tha' wha' I don' unnerstan! Bernie *was* ahead. He was winnin'! Had a few cuts n' bruises. Tim Sippowicz was a good boxer, mind ya, n' had gotten in some o' his combinations before Bernie got wise to 'im."

"So you're saying," Ben said, "that Bernie was okay when he went into the ninth?"

"Damn! He was great, rarin' to go! My cut man, Johnny Prospect, done a great job on a few cuts that the kid had, one on his forehead and one on the kid's cheek beside his left ear. I tell ya Bernie was like a man possessed when he went into the ninth!"

He looked at Maribeth. She was surprised at the emotional tone she heard in his voice.

"What time did ya say you found 'im?" Roscoe asked her.

"It was close to eleven."

"Left here right afta' the fight, round ten. Shouldna' taken 'im that long to get to the hospital. No more 'n twenty minutes. Wonda where he was all that time?"

There was silence in the room as the question lay unanswered.

Abruptly, his nervous tension mounting, Roscoe pushed back from the desk and got to his feet. He began to pace, lifting his feet and placing them down with a stickman stiffness. It was obvious to

Maribeth that the little man had something on his mind.

"Didn't go to his funeral mass," he said. He wiped his hand over his eyes and turned to Maribeth. "Guess I shoulda, but . . ." He sighed deeply. "Anyway, there's money owed 'im. Coupla thou' from the fight, ya know. His folks oughta get it, but I dunno how . . ."

Intuitively, Maribeth understood the manager's dilemma. Before Ben could stop her, she spoke up. "I'd be glad to let them know, Mr. Dunlap, if you want. Then you can mail the check to them."

"God, Maribeth!" Ben said to her as they left the seamy, shoddy building. "Why do you want to get so involved in this thing? I tell you, girl, you're heading into trouble."

"Not if I can find out the truth, Ben, what really happened to the man."

"So all right, what did you find out tonight?"

Maribeth understood Ben's concern. She was only a nurse, probably shouldn't even be trying to solve this problem, but she felt compelled somehow. So she tried to put Ben's mind at ease.

"I learned a few things, I think." She ticked them off on her fingers as Ben drove her home to her apartment.

"One, Roscoe Dunlap is worried. He was really fond of Bernie Hazzard. Two, he is afraid to face Bernie's parents. He knows something went wrong, that a healthy young man shouldn't die like that. He's worried something happened during the fight, something he should have seen, maybe between the eighth and ninth rounds. You heard him,

Ben, he said that Bernie went into the ninth like a 'man possessed.' I gathered from that that it was not his fighter's usual style. Think a stimulant of some sort could have been slipped into his drinking water?"

"Don't know, Maribeth. Do know I don't like what we're doing at all. Maybe I ought to let the precinct captain in on this."

"Wait, Ben." Maribeth placed her hand on his arm. "Wait. Not yet. We really have only suspicions now. My nursing experience tells me we have to have all the facts before we can make decisions—"

"And," he interrupted her bluntly, "my *police* training tells me we'd better let the police handle crimes. Oh, Maribeth," he pleaded, "let it go!"

"Need to find a few more answers, Ben. If it was murder, why . . . and who?"

"God, I don't know. People usually kill for love or money. Maybe both. I don't know. And, honey," he added cautiously, "have you thought of mob connections? I have, and I don't want you to be in danger."

"I know you're looking out for me, Ben, and I appreciate it. I know you are trying to protect me. Thanks."

She sat quietly as she watched Ben drive skillfully around Boston's busy streets. Her mind was busy as well.

"What if it was poison?"

"Well, wouldn't that poison expert from Washington have known that?"

"I don't really know," Maribeth mused. "You know, Ben, my father said something the other day. I was having dinner with my folks, took them some fresh vegetables and fruit from the D'Asardi farms. You know, Bernie's folks..."

"I know, you told me," Ben said dryly, as if he didn't want to talk about what she had done. "You really should stay away from that place."

"Well, anyway, we were talking about poisons and Dad said that there are poisons that people in *this* country don't even know about. He said all over the Caribbean many poisons are used by voodoo priests. Dad said he's been told that some work quickly on a person and others react slowly, over hours or days."

"And you believe something like that could have happened? Oh, Mari—"

Maribeth interrupted. "My mother agreed with Dad. She said in New Orleans, her home, a lot of that voodoo stuff goes on," she insisted.

"Well, I've never heard of anything like that going on in Boston. And believe me when I tell you, my dear girl, I've seen and heard plenty while I've been with the police. Plenty!" he emphasized.

Maribeth kept silent, thinking about what Ben had said. She had seen plenty tonight, too. There had been a tall, muscular, red-haired man over in a dark corner of the gym punching a speed bag. What was Dr. Peter Logan doing at the North End Gym?

Roscoe had another visitor later that night. One he was not at all happy to see, but one he had expected, sooner or later. Harry "the Hawk" was a member of a large mob that forced the local fight promoters to do business with them.

Harry's ambition was to move into the big time,

to control the local mob and move to even larger territory. He hoped to move in a wider circle someday, be his own boss, with his own mob.

The man's nickname came from his stark, cavernous physique. He was tall, thin, with licoricelike strands of black hair combed carefully over his bald head. His dark, heavily hooded eyes gave him a true hawkish appearance. Pure menace showed in the dour glower he afforded Roscoe that night.

"So, who were the jigs I saw you talkin' with?" he asked Roscoe right off.

He wasn't sure how much the Hawk knew about Bernie's death, but he suspected the mobster knew something. Roscoe shrugged his shoulders and spoke in an offhand way.

"Woman said she's the one who found Bernie . . . You heard what happened, found 'im on the hospital steps, and the guy, I don't know."

"Yeah, too bad 'bout Bernie," Harry replied. He compressed his thin lips into a tight line as if remembering something. "Seen that guy someplace before, though. So, wha'd ya tell 'em?"

Roscoe tried to cover up his nervousness. As usual, when flustered, he flung his hands into the air over his head.

"Nuthin'! I told 'em nuthin'. What could I tell 'em?"

"Right," the Hawk concurred. "Jes' be careful who ya talk to, tha's all. Rock"—got right to the point—"I'm collectin' tonight."

"I got ya money," Roscoe said soberly.

"That's real good, Rocky. Real good."

Roscoe rose from his chair, went to his safe, and handed a packet of bills to the Hawk. If there was only some way he could be free of this blackmailing gangster, he thought wearily as he watched Harry count out the weekly thousand dollars Roscoe paid him. Harry Holtz stuffed the money in his inside coat pocket and started to leave. He snapped his fingers. "Say, I think I know where I seen that colored guy before—municipal court, downtown. Could be a cop or a lawyer. Rock, be careful who you talk to," he warned.

"Yeah, right," Roscoe answered. Right now he wished there *was* someone who could help him.

A few days later Maribeth drove to Concord to visit the D'Asardis and to tell them about the money owed to their son. At first Salvatore D'Asardi resisted.

"I jes' wanna know who killed my kid. Can't think about money. No way!" he said bitterly.

But Rini D'Asardi reacted differently.

"Sal," she implored her husband, "Bernie would want you to have the money."

"No, no," he said. "No money, Rini."

Her husband thundered out of the living room, his massive shoulders hunched up around his neck. His pain was obvious. When he reached the patio door, he stopped. "Do what you want, Rini," he flung over his shoulder as he strode out to the patio. Through the glass doors Maribeth saw him sink into a chair, his head in his hands.

Mrs. D'Asardi gave Maribeth a weak smile as they both watched the stricken man.

"He's still so upset, my husband, but life must go on, eh, Miss Trumbull? I try to be strong for him."

"It's all you can do, I guess, Mrs. D'Asardi."

The woman walked over to the door of the sunroom as if she wanted to comfort her husband. Then she stopped and turned resolutely toward Maribeth.

"So tell Mr. Roscoe Dunlap to send the check for Bernie's money, made out to me, Rini D'Asardi..." Her voice faltered. "Bernie's..." She could scarcely say the word *mother*.

Her dark eyes filled with tears that spilled down her cheeks.

"We still have another son, Miss Trumbull. He's only sixteen, can't take Bernie's place, but he's a good boy, too. Always wanted to go to art school. I was afraid the army would take them, but my boys had farm deferments as long as they stayed on the farm. But I know he's restless. Maybe now..."

She left her thought unfinished, but Maribeth felt she understood. Mrs. D'Asardi was a mother. Her sons came first. It was almost as if the older son were giving something to his younger brother. Perhaps the money would help him get into art school.

Maribeth felt rested after a few days off and signed up with the nurses' registry for a new case.

"We have a young mother at Zion Memorial, emergency hysterectomy, uterus ruptured during delivery," Maribeth was told by the registry. She agreed to take the case, eleven P.M. to seven A.M., beginning tonight.

When she went into Hanna Peters's room that night, she found her patient still receiving a blood transfusion. She had lost a great deal of blood during her emergency surgery. But she was still in an excitable state.

"How do you feel, Mrs. Peters?" Maribeth asked

the young mother. Her dark curly hair spilled out over the pillow and she gave Maribeth a triumphant smile.

"Oh, nurse, I'm fine! I've got two beautiful babies!"

"Two?" Maribeth questioned. She'd been told there was only one Peters baby, a boy, doing quite well in the intensive care nursery.

"Oh no, only one! But what I meant was I found out I was pregnant the same day I brought my first baby home. Neil was only two days old when we got him. After four years of trying, we adopted. Then, that day, we found out we were having Joshua! I'm so happy . . . can't have any more . . . but I'm satisfied with my two sons!"

"You're very lucky," Maribeth agreed as she busied herself checking the young mother's condition. Her mind raced back to Rini D'Asardi. She also had been the mother of two sons.

After a quiet night—the exhausted young mother had slept through most of it—Maribeth was still alert when she arrived home that morning. She decided to get right to bed anyway. Her mind was racing with thoughts of the Hazzard mystery but her body needed to relax. She did feel a degree of tension, like waiting for the other shoe to drop.

She took a warm relaxing bath, slid in between cool sheets in her shade-drawn room, and settled down. She was almost asleep when the phone rang. Damn, another telephone salesman.

"Hello?" she dragged out sleepily.

"Miss Maribeth Trumbull?"

"Yes."

"If you don't want to find another body, maybe yours this time, back off."

"Who . . . who is this?" Maribeth answered.

She heard only a click, then the hum of the dead telephone line.

Fully awake now, Maribeth was really frightened for the first time since she had involved herself in the Bernie Hazzard case. Now someone knew where she lived, and to make matters worse, her old car had been giving her trouble.

Only two nights ago she had been on her way to ZMH when the car sputtered and stalled. Luckily she was near an all-night gas station.

"Oh my, you're in big trouble," the mechanic had said from under the hood as he examined her car.

"But can you fix it for me? I must get to the hospital as soon as I can."

"Do the best I can, ma' am. You know how it is with these old cars, 'specially now with the war an' all."

He continued to grunt and shake his head as Maribeth waited. She wondered if she should call the hospital to tell them she might be late. That was certainly the last thing she wanted to do. But maybe . . . She was about to inquire about a telephone when the mechanic emerged from under the hood, slammed it shut, wiped his hands on a greasy rag, and made his pronouncement.

"You're all set, ma'am. That will be ten dollars, please."

Relieved that she would make it to her patient on time, Maribeth handed the man a ten-dollar bill. *He must have X-ray eyes,* she thought. It was all the money she had in her purse with the exception of some loose change.

The following evening she had had dinner with

her parents and she had told her father about the car incident.

"I'll take a look, honey," he had reassured her. "Car's running all right otherwise?"

"Yes, it is, Dad."

Her father returned to the kitchen in a few minutes.

"Come on out to the garage with me, Mari, want to show you something."

He had moved his car out of the one car garage, had driven her car inside. Under the lights he pointed to something under the raised hood.

"See here, child?" He showed her a small round cap that had wires protruding from beneath it. "This is a distributor cap. See these steel spring clamps that hold it down?"

Maribeth nodded.

"The distributor cap," her father explained, "has wires that are part of the ignition system of a car. It is the device that applies electric current in the right sequence to the spark plugs. Now see here." He showed her a clamp that was hanging loose. "Sometimes these clamps lose their tension and pop loose, loosening the cap and the wires."

"So what do I do if this happens again?"

"I've bent some of the clamps to make them tighter, but as soon as I can I'll try to find you a new cap. Okay?"

"Gee, Dad, thanks a lot."

"No problem. Got to look out for my baby."

What would her father have said if she had told him about the anonymous call? She had decided she wouldn't tell him, but she had to tell Ben.

She got out of bed, showered, and dressed because she and Ben were having dinner tonight. She tried to do a little studying, but found herself too nervous to do so. What had she stumbled into? What should she do now? *Ben will be furious! He's probably right. But, "in for a penny, in for a pound,"* she thought. *Can't stop now.*

Seven

Ben brought Chinese food to Maribeth's apartment that evening. They had agreed that was a comfortable way for them to be together since they both worked the night tour. Maribeth had arranged the cartons of chicken chow mein, fried scallops, and shrimp-fried rice on the coffee table in front of her radio. The news commentator was talking about the Dunbarton Oaks conference that opened at Washington, D.C., with delegates from the United States, England, China, and Russia establishing proposals for the United Nations.

"There's got to be a way to settle disputes. Countries can't keep having wars," Ben commented as he helped himself to more shrimp-fried rice. "I mean, people should be more civilized."

Maribeth murmured an agreement, her mind on the reaction she expected to receive when she told Ben about the phone call. She knew she had to tell him. Now was as good a time as any. So without a preface she put her plate on the table and plunged right into her unpalatable news.

"I got a phone call this morning. Some man threatened my life if I didn't back off from..."

Ben dropped his forkful of food, which was halfway to his mouth, leaped to his feet, and glared at Maribeth. His mouth released his angry words with a vehemence that made her cringe. She stepped back involuntarily, away from his palpable anger. Ben saw her move, recovered quickly, and reached for her to gather her protectively close.

"God damn it, Maribeth! I told you not to meddle in this! Now look what's happened!" He wiped his mouth with a napkin and flung it angrily on top of the opened food cartons. He strode around the room, returned to stand in front of Maribeth, and with his forefinger jabbed the air in front of her face.

"Damn! Now someone knows where you live, your phone number, where you work, most likely . . . You're in danger! You don't know what kind of nuts are out there! Damn it to hell, girl, why'd you have to poke your nose in something you don't know anything about?"

Maribeth kept silent because she knew Ben was right. She was in over her head, but somehow she couldn't back away. Her curiosity wouldn't let her stop now.

Ben was still talking. He spoke with deep concern, Maribeth heard it in his tone of voice.

"This will have to be reported to the precinct captain. He's going to chew me out for this, and he'll be right. Know why?"

She shrugged.

"He'll be right because I know better. I've been trained better. Call myself a professional police officer and let my girlfriend mess around with something she shouldn't," he muttered.

Maribeth kept silent. This turn of events meant something had to change, she realized that. She got up from the couch and began to clean up. Neither of them seemed to want to continue eating. Ben carried the dirty dishes into the kitchen and put them in the sink. He turned from the sink to face Maribeth as she brought the empty teacups in.

"I'll be all right. Listen—"

Ben shook his head.

"That's what I've been doing all along, listening to you, my girl, but now that's over! You're going to listen to me."

"Well, where am I going to go?" Maribeth questioned. "If I go home to Cambridge, my folks will want to know why. I haven't lived home for some time now. I can't go back home! And they'd be so worried, too."

"You could stay with me," Ben ventured, "but I know you don't want to do that . . . Course I'd like it. Tell you what, the Jefferson Terrace House rents rooms to young women, you can stay there."

Jefferson Terrace House was a large brick hotel for single, career-minded women who came to Boston to further their education and/or careers. It was considered safe for young women, and rooms could be rented by the day, week, or month. Most of the guests were transient, but there were older women who made Jefferson Terrace House their home. Some were elderly spinsters who had lived there for years. They tried to mother the younger women. A few girls tolerated the interest, others did not. Maribeth knew she wouldn't mind the maternal attention.

She knew, too, that Ben was right. She would not be safe in her apartment until this mess was cleared up. And, she had to admit, she was glad Ben was looking out for her.

She gave the nursing directory the number where she could be reached, explaining that it was a temporary one. And she took Ben's advice. She did not accept any more cases at Zion Memorial.

"I think you'd better stay away from there until this thing blows over," he advised. She agreed and asked the directory for cases at Massachusetts General, Brigham and Women's, or Mount Auburn in Cambridge. When she was at Mount Auburn, she could stop and have breakfast with her parents. Sometimes she'd even sleep over in her old room. Both parents accepted her explanation for being home more frequently.

"Mrs. Edson is having my apartment done over," she explained to her parents, hoping that the lie would never surface. She hated to lie, especially to her parents.

That night at dinner, as if he knew what was on her mind, her father brought up the subject of secret societies and strange poisons used in their rituals.

"You know, honey," he said, "here in America we don't think such things can happen. But, truly, anywhere you get a gathering of folks from the old country, there's plenty of them believe that 'poison voodoo' stuff."

Her mother agreed, adding, "Even my own grandmere from over St. Constant's way could find a root, an herb, leaves, twigs, fix you up a paste or drink that could cure anything from toothache, toe ache, or help you 'drop a baby' if you was of a mind to."

"I've heard that there are lots of things . . ."

"Sure, Maribeth, from spiderwebs to ground-up fish scales to the bark of the willow tree," her father added. "But really, I think a lot of it is in the person's mind."

"Not necessarily, Dad," Maribeth argued. "A poison will affect the body itself whether or not the victim has a sound mind or not. It's the reaction of a chemical on the body's tissues, I think."

"Could be," Maribeth's father said. "But don't you take any chances. Especially going to work at night. It's a rough world out there," he cautioned.

If only you knew, Maribeth thought.

She had signed on with a case of a young suicidal college student at Massachusetts General Hospital. The student had crumbled under the weight of adjusting to a new and different world of college at Radcliffe and had tried to commit suicide by overdosing on her tranquilizers.

Maribeth had been warned that not only had the patient tried to kill herself, but threatened to kill anyone who tried to intervene. She was going to be flown back to her home in Buenos Aires the next morning.

Maribeth monitored the patient closely. The young woman had been placed in restraints for her own protection and for those whom she had threatened. Maribeth's orders were to keep the patient under sedation.

Relieved that it had been an uneventful night and that her prayers for a peaceful night had been answered, she hurried the next morning to her car in the parking lot, anxious to get to Jefferson Terrace House before the morning commuting traffic became heavy.

"Morning, Miss Trumbull. Haven't seen you over at Zion Memorial for a while. Given up on us?"

Maribeth looked at the person who had spoken.

He was dressed in a dark suit but she recognized the wiry red hair of the muscular young man that she had last seen when he pronounced her patient, Mr. Prescott.

"Oh, good morning, Dr. Logan."

"Working here at MGH, I see."

"Yes. I had a case here last night."

"Is that right? Well, we miss you at Zion, Miss Trumbull. Hope you haven't deserted us." He smiled.

"Not at all, Doctor. I just go wherever I get a case," Maribeth explained.

"I see. Well, I'm on my way to a seminar here this morning. Dr. Sandifer is giving an update on the pacemaker he's been working on. The man's a genius, you know."

"He really is, Dr. Logan, he certainly is."

"Hope to see you back at Zion, Miss Trumbull. Soon." He ran briskly up the front stairs of the building.

She unlocked her car door and got in, threw her bag and sweater on the front seat. Funny thing, she thought, running into Peter Logan like that. She'd wondered about him since seeing him that time at Roscoe's gym. Did he have anything to do . . . with anything? She turned the key in the ignition and decided perhaps she'd ask him. There might be a simple explanation with nothing at all to do with the boxer's unfortunate death.

Peter Logan, M.D., frowned as he watched Maribeth walk through the parking lot to her Chevy. It was a blue sedan. He couldn't read the license plate from where he stood behind a large post, but he felt he'd certainly recognize the car again. He spotted a dingy yellow plastic flower that waved from the radio antenna as Maribeth drove away. So, she had been avoiding Zion Memorial Hospital. He wondered why. He wondered, too, what was a young colored nurse doing at a boxing gym, especially a seedy, run-down place like Rocky's?

In the brief time he'd been an intern at Zion, he'd learned who the good, efficient nurses were, and she was one of them. He remembered the way she had fought for Ned Prescott's life. The pacemaker he was going to hear more about today probably would have saved the man's life. It was times like that when a doctor felt helpless, when he saw life slip away. He found his way to the lecture hall and got a seat. What he learned today might make a difference. He hoped so.

Maribeth had a hard time sleeping that day, and when she finally managed to drop off, her dreams were disturbing. There were patients in short johnnies running up and down hospital corridors, laughing at her while she tried to get them back into their beds, some with gaping wounds on their heads, stomachs, some hopping on too-short crutches so that the patients looked hunched over like dwarfs. Maribeth woke up in a cold sweat. Maybe Ben was right. Perhaps she was in this over her head, but she had never been a quitter and she couldn't stop now. She had to find out all she could about the boxer's death. There's a reason for everything. Things don't just happen. There has to be a cause and a resulting response to that cause. All of her training and education had taught her that.

She had to admit to herself that taking care of that psychotic patient hadn't done much for her nerves.

She decided to go shopping at Filene's Basement. There was a sale on raincoats and her old one no longer repelled the rain. She found a nice navy one, size ten, and the price was good. Filene's Basement was notorious for not having dressing rooms for customers to try on merchandise. The marketing system was you tried things on right where you stood. Women tried on blouses and skirts right over the clothing that they were wearing. So Maribeth took off her coat, threw it over the coatrack, and with her pocketbook between her legs tried on the new raincoat. It was a well-known brand name and it fit perfectly. She was satisfied with it, so she took it off, put on her coat, and went to the nearest clerk to pay for it. She was leaving the basement on her way to the street level when she sensed that someone was moving very close behind her. Fear rose in her throat but she didn't want to turn around in a confrontation. If she could get to her car in the parking lot near Summer Street, she'd be safe. She hurried along. On the sidewalk she quickened her steps and almost panicked when she heard the footsteps behind her speed up to the same pace as her own. She grasped her keys in her coat pocket, the familiar-shaped metal reassuring her. *At least they're handy, and if only I get to the car, I'll be safe.* Intent on getting to safety, she scurried along the sidewalk, oblivious of the people who crowded the busy shopping area. Her skin erupted in goose bumps and she felt the prickle of hair stand up on her neck. The car! The car! Where had she parked it? Then she remembered, A-level, just beyond the stairs. By now she was running as she entered the parking plaza. She wasn't sure if her assailant was running behind her, but she knew she had to move quickly. She did not see the man until he stepped out from the front of the car and grabbed her arms.

"Ben! Oh my God, you scared me to death!" she choked. "There's a man!" She peered backward, safe in Ben's strong arms. "A man was following me! Oh, Ben, I was so scared!" He held her close as she drew in deep breaths.

"I know," Ben said. "I saw him. I think it was a mobster they call the Hawk. I've seen him in court plenty of times. *Now,*" he said firmly, "little Miss would-be-nurse-detective, *we* are going to see the captain. No ifs, ands, buts, or maybes!"

Still shaken by the encounter, Maribeth was happy to hand the car keys over to Ben, who got behind the wheel. With expert ease he drove out of the parking plaza onto the busy street.

"Ben, that must mean that somehow the mob had something to do with Bernie Hazzard's death, don't you think?"

"Maribeth, I don't know . . ." Ben's voice trailed with worry. "Could be, but we're seeing the captain tomorrow, first thing. We'll let the police handle this, okay?"

Ben was not only tired of the whole thing, but he was worried. No one fooled with the mobsters, especially those mob members who lived by the "code of silence." They were extremely dangerous. But what was even more dangerous was facing his superior.

Captain Tom Curry ran a tight ship. Everything was done by the book. He knew police procedure and meticulously followed it.

The next morning Ben and Maribeth kept their appointment with the precinct captain. Ben was very nervous, Maribeth could see, but he maintained his composure and spoke to his commanding officer in a firm voice.

"Good morning, sir."

"Good morning, Sergeant."

"Miss Trumbull and I have some information that we believe may be pertinent in the investigation of the boxer's death."

"That so?" The captain raised an eyebrow. "Please go on. One moment."

He buzzed for his secretary and a young woman in a police uniform came in and took a seat beside his desk.

"We need to take down your statement," he explained to Maribeth.

"I understand, sir," she said and she looked toward Ben.

"Miss Trumbull's life has been threatened and someone has been following her."

The captain nodded, turned his attention to Ben. Beads of sweat had formed on Ben's upper lip and forehead and Maribeth realized that she shared considerable responsibility for her friend's discomfort. There was no mistaking the captain's displeasure at his officer.

"Just promoted to sergeant, right, Daniels?" he said sarcastically as he shuffled through some papers on his desk. "Did you forget everything you've learned? I could, by rights, bust you right back to patrolman; interfering in police work, withholding evidence . . . You've got yourself in some trouble. You know you're never to let a civilian tell you how to do police work. Now your friend here is in physical danger..."

Maribeth knew Ben was uncomfortable, but he showed no signs of wilting under his superior's condemnation. He spoke up quickly.

"I'm aware of my responsibilities, sir. Mainly I wanted to help Miss Trumbull look out for her—"

"By interfering in a police investigation?" the captain broke in.

"I did not see it as interfering, sir," Ben insisted. "No information has ever been withheld from the police by us. Citizens do have the right to seek information as long as they don't impede an investigation being conducted by the police."

Maribeth looked at Ben. What she saw impressed her. His serious persistence was revealed by the reddened flush on his face. She also heard determination in his voice. Despite the fact that he was speaking to a superior officer, he was willing to risk all to defend her. Her admiration for him increased.

"So... she had come forward of her own accord to offer information she has. She wants to assist the police in any way possible," Ben continued.

"Not to mention that she has been threatened—"

"Captain Curry," Maribeth broke in. "It's my fault, sir, for being so stubborn and so curious. I should have listened to Sergeant Daniels but I wanted to find out what I could," she persisted. "I did learn that the medical examiner is not sure of the cause of death. Thinks it may be an exotic poison of some kind—"

Captain Curry raised his hand to stop Maribeth's comments.

"Miss Trumbull, do I have to remind you again that this is an official police matter? We do know how to do our job, miss, as I am sure you know how to do your nursing. You stick to that and leave the police work to us. If we need your nursing expertise, we'll call you. You've moved temporarily, I take it?"

"Yes, sir, to Jefferson Terrace House."

"Good." He turned to Ben. "Sergeant Daniels, I'm sure you know that today's meeting and the resulting decisions will be entered in your personnel file."

"Yes, sir."

Maribeth's face flushed as she heard the superior officer chastise Ben. She realized that because of her headstrong actions, plus her relationship to Ben, facts had been presented that could possibly besmirch Ben's heretofore unblemished police career. She would have to make amends, somehow. It wasn't Ben's fault.

They left the precinct station house, relieved to be out in the welcome sunshine. Ben was deeply concerned. Maribeth could see that as he helped her into his car and started the engine. He moved the car slowly into traffic.

"Ben, will this mean a black mark on your record? I mean, the captain was very angry, I could tell. I'm really sorry . . . should have listened to you . . ."

"There will probably be a reprimand or a lower rating in my next evaluation. Or the captain may figure on something else. I don't know. Have to wait and see, I guess."

"I'm so sorry, Ben. Really I am. Like I said before, I guess I should have listened to you. Do you think the police do have a handle on this mystery?"

"My God, Maribeth," Ben sputtered. "What's with you? In one breath you tell me you're sorry for the trouble you've got me into and in the next breath you are still concerned about something you have *no* business thinking about! I'm not thinking about what the police are doing about this stinkin' murder! I'm only trying to keep you safe and also protect my job! All right?" He pleaded with her, his attention distracted momentarily by the traffic. "Leave it alone, please, Maribeth!"

"Yes, Ben, I will. I promise."

Her fingers were crossed behind her back where Ben couldn't see them.

Rini D'Asardi decided that she wanted to visit the North End Gym where her son had spent the last hours of his life, also to pick up his belongings. Maribeth agreed to drive her there. She had a few unanswered questions of her own that she wanted to clear up. She did not tell Ben. The way she saw it, she was helping a grieving mother trying to come to grips with her son's death. And if, in doing so, she found the answers to a few questions as well, so be it.

She decided to let Roscoe know that they were coming. She telephoned him.

"Will you get Bernie's belongings together, Mr. Dunlap? His mother would like to have them."

"Yeah, okay, I'll have the stuff ready for ya."

"Thanks, Mr. Dunlap. Don't think Mrs. D'Asardi will want to stay very long. So if you have everything ready we'll just come in and pick it up."

"You know, Miss Trumbull—"

"Maribeth, please, Mrs. D'Asardi," Maribeth said as later that afternoon they drove to the north end of Boston.

"Maribeth, it's such a pretty name, and you're a pretty girl, too."

"Thanks, Mrs. D'Asardi, you're very kind," Maribeth answered as she maneuvered around the busy traffic on Embankment Road.

"I wanted to tell you, Maribeth, that Sal and I lived one time in the North End before we bought the farm in Concord. 'Little Italy,' they call it. We were happy there, my Sal and I. What I wanted to tell you, Maribeth, is that the North End is where I grew up."

"Really?"

"Yes, and it's where I met Sal. We were sweethearts, even though he's older." She laughed softly. "He's the first man I ever kissed."

"You love him very much."

"I do, and I need to help him. We'll never get over losing Bernie, I know that, but I've got to help him find peace somehow."

Maribeth looked over at the middle-aged woman sitting beside her. She wore a black suit, and a small black hat sat perched on her dark hair. With some small gesture to modern American life, uncharacteristically, she wore her hair in short crisp curls, which gave her a youthful appearance. Her black-gloved hands clenched her pocketbook. Occasionally she stared out of the car window and remarked once on the many changes she saw.

"You're right," Maribeth told her. "I think Boston is trying to move into the twenty-first century with new hotels and stuff. The war is bound to be over soon and things will start booming. Well, here we are," she said as she pulled up in front of the old two-story building. "Sure you want to go in, Mrs. D'Asardi?"

"North End Gym," the woman said. She shook her head grimly. "Yes, I must go in. I have to . . . for Bernie and for Sal."

Maribeth was surprised by what she saw. Today there was no activity. The windows along the side of the large room had been opened and the afternoon sun poured in like molten gold over the wooden floor. A gentle breeze of soft warm air gave the room a special peaceful feeling. The speed bags and punching bags hung limply along the inner wall as if relieved to be quiet and resting.

Roscoe Dunlap came out of his corner office when he saw the two women walk across the gym floor.

Maribeth couldn't believe it was the same little man she'd seen a few nights before. Dressed in a dark suit and tie, he came forward, extended his hand to Rini D'Asardi. "Very sorry about Bernie, ma'am."

"Thank you," Mrs. D'Asardi answered.

"I have your son's things right here," he said as he led them into his office. That room, too, Maribeth saw, had been cleaned up. She looked around the room, quickly noting that Bernie's picture had been removed. That was considerate, Maribeth thought.

"It's all in this box, ma'am," Roscoe said, indicating a cardboard box on his desk. "Mostly his gear, sweatpants, jerseys, mouthpiece, gloves, coupla pair of shorts, towels, and a toilet kit. Stuff like that he had in his locker."

Rini D'Asardi gently fingered the toilet kit as she and Maribeth looked at the items Roscoe mentioned.

"His father gave him that traveling kit years ago," she said. "When he started boxing."

Maribeth glanced at the array of articles. Ordinary stuff, she thought. Then her eyes gravitated to a small white jar that she saw was labeled *cut salve*. *I wonder if it contains coagulants, medication to stop bleeding*. Despite her promise to Ben, she knew she'd have to find out.

Maribeth decided that it would be best if they left as soon as possible. She could see that Bernie's mother was beginning to struggle with her emotions as she looked at what remained of her son's life. "Would you like a receipt for this, Mr. Dunlap?" Maribeth asked.

"Guess so, just in case . . ." the man mumbled.

Maribeth wrote out a few lines stating that Bernie Hazzard's personal belongings had been picked up by his mother. She dated the note and signed it, then handed it to Mrs. D'Asardi for her signature. While the woman was reading and signing the receipt, Maribeth asked Roscoe the question that had been plaguing her for days.

"Do you know Peter Logan, Mr. Dunlap?"

"You mean *Dr.* Peter Logan?" His eyes brightened up. It was obvious he was glad to change the subject. "Been knowing him since he was a snot-nosed kid running in here begging me for a job cleaning up, actin' as water boy, sparring as he got older. Everybody here knows Peter Logan and his old man, too, Dennis Logan. The old man used to put on the gloves once in a while, but he was never as good as his son."

"So Dr. Logan still comes here sometimes?"

"He's not the type of guy that forgits where he started. Comes here to work out. Says he gits ridda stress, don'cha kno?" Roscoe seemed to warm to his story. "One helluva guy . . . made somepin' o' himself. You know 'im?"

"We've worked together at the hospital."

"Oh, right, I forgit you're a nurse."

And Maribeth thought, *I can't wait to get my hands on that cut salve.* She had a good friend in the medical lab at the state police lab. Ira Dohain was in her psych class. He'd run some tests for her.

One of the young nurses who consistently worked the night-duty shift as a private nurse was getting married.

There was a special camaraderie among the private-duty night nurses. Always willing to help with each other's patients, they were close and shared their lives with one another. The young bride had invited many of her coworkers to her wedding, and Maribeth was one of them.

"Can I bring my boyfriend?" she asked the bride-to-be, a spirited, vivacious, friendly Italian-American girl whose answer came quickly.

"Of course, of course. I'm dying to meet that policeman friend of yours!"

It was during the ceremony that Maribeth began to realize how important Ben Daniels had become to her. How much she was beginning to depend on him. How solicitous he was about her welfare. She glanced at him and noticed how intently he was observing the ceremony. He must have sensed her eyes on him because he looked at her, smiled, and reached for her hand. He did not let go until the ceremony was concluded.

The reception was held in a large hall that contained an elegant wide staircase with one of the largest chandeliers in New England.

Maribeth was impressed and almost overwhelmed by the warmth and exuberance of her friend's large Italian family. Somehow her thoughts returned to the grieving D'Asardi family. Was there a chance *they* might have this kind of joy with their remaining son? Somehow an instant brief chill over her body warned her that they would not. There was something about young Louis that gave Maribeth strong doubts.

Eight

"Dennis Sean Michael Logan! You're *not* going near Suffolk Downs! Indeed not!"

Dennis Logan did not mistake the anger and indignation of his wife. He knew she was upset, this time more than usual. He could see it in her manner, hands akimbo on her hips. He heard it in her strident voice as she positioned herself in front of the back door when he started to leave.

She was a tiny woman, only five feet, in comparison to her six-foot tall, muscular, red-haired husband. But what she lacked in physical characteristics she more than made up for in courage and tenacity.

"Dennis," she warned, pointing and gesturing with her finger in his face, "go to the track today and I'm warnin' you, you'll come home to an empty house!"

She glared at her husband, her deep blue eyes turned almost stone black with anger, her usually milk-white fair Irish complexion mottled with red blotches as her temper exploded. Tension in the room hung between them like a smothering thick cloud.

"I'll not be here! Now this time is the last. I've had it with your gamblin'!"

Dennis reached for her to take her in his arms.

"Oh, Ellen, love," he pleaded, "'tis a sure thing I'm bettin' on this time, true as God."

"You needn't be bringin' the Almighty into this, Dennis Logan, not at all. Though He knows 'tis me that's been pleadin' with Him all these years to rid you of this dreadful curse." She threw up her hands, made her way into their living room, almost as if she could not bear to be near him.

Since they had met as high school teenagers in south Boston, gambling had been an undying passion for Dennis and an ever-present burden for Ellen. Dennis would bet on anything, from the number of inches of snow that would fall on a winter's day to the number of home runs the home run king would score in a given game.

Ellen knew her husband loved her. He tried to give her everything she wanted. Whenever he won, whether at cards, pool, a pinball machine, or at the races, he would bring his winnings home to her. "All for you, Ellen, my love," he would say.

This day she stood her ground.

"Dennis, you're not a young man anymore." Her voice was quiet and serious, matter-of-fact and passionless. Some of the mottled red blotches had faded from her face. Instead, it was chalk white as she presented her case.

"I'm not young anymore, either, Dennis. 'Tis a good thing our only child is a doctor, praise God, and can fend for himself. You know all we've got is each other. We could make it, too, with your railroad pension. Thank God you can't touch that. We could make out if only you'd quit gamblin'. Can't you see that?"

Her voice softened as she watched her husband's

MEANT TO BE

face. "You've always been a good husband, my love. Always worked hard every day at the railroad yard, but it was always the weekends that got me, Dennis; never knowing if you'd be off gamblin' at the pool hall, the racetrack, the boxing gym, or whatever . . ."

Her eyes narrowed with intensity as she watched her husband's restless response to her sad litany. "Dennis Sean Michael, you're the only man I've ever loved, and I always will, too, till the day I die, but . . ." Her voice cracked.

"Ellen, Ellen." Dennis gathered her close in his arms. "This is the last time, I promise. . . ."

"You *always* promise," she mumbled into his chest. Her tears, flowing freely now, sprinkled his shirt as she clung to him.

His thoughts increased the panic he experienced. Please, God, Ellen should never find out how desperate he was this day. Harry the Hawk had seen to that.

"So, you're puttin' money on Bernie Hazzard," the mobster had taunted Dennis.

As the Hawk had expected, Dennis Logan's ego was aroused and he was visibly excited by the hoodlum's challenge.

"Sure I am!"

The Hawk smiled, pulled a cigar from his inside coat pocket, tore away the cellophane, cut off the end, and expertly rolled it over his tongue. His eyes never left Dennis Logan's face.

He was anxious to bait Dennis into a big wager. "Think he can take Sippowicz, the champ?"

"And why not?" Dennis demanded, excited by the prospect of a sizable wager, a chance to really clean up, score big. He would be able to retire early, take his Ellen to Ireland for a visit he'd always promised her.

"Think the kid's got a chance?" Harry taunted.

"Damn straight!" Dennis retorted quickly. "I've known the kid since he was in diapers. Him and my own Peter were born the same day, it was, an' growin' up together, boxin' in the North End Gym . . . Why shouldn't I put my money on the kid? Sure to be the next middleweight champion." Warmed to his subject, Dennis continued expansively, "He'll take Tim Sippowicz by the fourth round, my money's on it."

"You're sure of that?" the Hawk persisted.

"Ah." Dennis shook his head slowly, his lips turned down with cynical contempt. "The Polock kid maybe okay, but he doesn't have the skills and the ring savvy of my lad Bernie. No way," he said.

That was two weeks ago and Dennis had been duly warned. The Hawk wanted his money no later than two days from now. With his silently weeping wife in his arms, Dennis was worried. He could not bring himself to tell her the truth, that their home was no longer theirs. When Bernie Hazzard lost the fight, the property, all that they owned, belonged to Harry the Hawk. Dennis knew this was his last chance. He had to go to the track one more time. If he could hit the daily double, win a bundle, he could pay off the Hawk. He was due for a win, and in his bones he truly felt today was the day. Despite Ellen's dire warning, he had to go to the track. Just had to.

"On my mother's grave, Ellen, love, I swear this is the last time." He saw the anger spark again in her eyes. She shook her remaining tears from her eyes and this time there was a slight tremor in her voice though she spoke slowly, with serious intent.

"After thirty-five years, you're damn right it's the last time . . . I won't be here when you get back."

"Oh, Ellen, don't, don't talk such nonsense. You don't mean that."

"But I do, Dennis, as much as I've ever meant anything in my life."

Peter Logan had the weekend off. He telephoned Rayna.

"I'm beat down, my love, after ninety-six hours on duty. I need to crash somewhere. But before I can reach your loving arms, I have to check on Ma."

"When can I expect you, Pete?" his girlfriend asked.

"It's noon now. I've just signed off I'll get right over to my folks' house. Maybe spend a couple of hours . . . should be in Worcester by four or so."

"I'll be waiting."

"Great, hon. See you soon."

Hard work was never a problem for Peter Logan. He relished the challenges it provided. Ever since his sophomore year in high school he had worked; after school at a diner and summers at a local greenhouse. He worked while attending college, telling his proud parents, "Don't need your money. Do it on my own." Even in medical school he was not happy if he didn't have a job on the side.

The piano lessons his mother had insisted upon came in handy and with some of his friends he formed a little combo. They made extra money playing local gigs on free weekends.

He'd been able to purchase a little pickup truck

that was put into service when friends needed to move furniture from one apartment to the other. He was driving the vehicle now on his way home to check on his mother.

He sighed as he drove along Boston's old streets. He knew he was doing well in his internship; the attendings and senior staff physicians had welcomed him, commented on his quick diagnostic perception, his take-charge decision making, and indicated he might be a candidate for a residency appointment when his internship was completed. He knew he was learning a great deal. His future seemed bright. He and Rayna had an understanding, but now this problem with his dad . . .

It always seemed to happen, just when things were on an even keel, his father had impulsively gambled away his pay. Peter and his mother would have to scrounge around to pay whatever bill loomed with a past-due note stamped on it.

Peter loved his father, knew he was a good man, but this overwhelming sickness, this severe gambling habit for which his son, Peter Logan, M.D., had yet to find a cure . . . Maybe, if his mother did leave his father . . . He wondered as he drove into the familiar driveway.

Peter found his mother in tears.

"Your da has done it again," she said in a soft, weepy brogue. "Can't keep him away from the gamblin'. Told him I'd not be here when he got back, but where am I goin'?" she sobbed.

Peter believed in action. "Put your coat and hat on, Ma. You're coming with me. You can stay with Rayna, my girlfriend."

"Oh, Peter, I don't like the sound of that. I'd never want to interfere in your affairs. Never!"

"God, you're my mother, and it's *not* interfering," Peter insisted. "Rayna and I have an understanding. She'll be glad to help out in our little crisis."

"Well, maybe for a day or so, until I can figure what to do about your da. Seems we've come to a crossroad, we have."

"Don't worry, Ma, everything's going to be fine."

He knew that Rayna had an extra bedroom in her apartment, one of many three-decker houses in the city owned by her father.

Rayna Genrose welcomed Peter's mother.

"It's nice to see you again, Mrs. Logan. Come in, please, and make yourself comfortable."

"I told Peter I didn't want to be a bother." Mrs. Logan's flushed face revealed her anxiety.

"Oh, you're not a bother at all, Mrs. Logan."

"But I shouldn't be here, shouldn't interfere—"

"Ma! Ma! Look, it's all right!" Peter interrupted. "Rayna's glad to help out."

"Well, maybe, for a minute, till I can catch me breath."

"Come with me, Mrs. Logan. I've got a little guest room where you can put your feet up and rest. I'm going to make a pot of tea. Would you like a cup?"

"If it's not too much trouble."

"No trouble at all." Rayna looked over the troubled woman's head to see Peter clasping his hands together in a gesture of thanks. She led the still protesting woman down the hall.

Peter sat down on the couch. He always felt relaxed in Rayna's cheerfully decorated living room. Vibrant blues and greens patterned the sofa. Plain soft muslin pillows placed along the back of the couch created a restful setting.

Rayna's green thumb was evidenced by the

healthy, flourishing plants that hung in the large bay window behind the sofa. It formed an oasis of peace and tranquillity. An old-fashioned bentwood rocker had been placed to the right of the couch. Her mother had knit a black and white afghan, which lay across one arm of the rocker. On the other side of the couch was an overstuffed chair with a matching ottoman. It was Peter's favorite.

Peter heard the loving, sincere tone in Rayna's voice as she tried to ease his mind.

"I've settled your mother in the back bedroom, with a cup of hot tea, her feet up on a hassock, and the radio tuned to her favorite soap opera. She seems comfortable."

"Thanks, hon. Guess I'd better check on the old man." He sighed. "This thing about Da's gambling has been a problem since I was a kid. Maybe this time, when he finds out Ma is serious about leaving him . . ."

"There's a wall phone in the kitchen, you know, Pete. Use that one."

"Yes, Da, it's me, Pete."

"By God, Pete, 'tis a good thing you called. You know, your ma's not here at home! Don't know where she's gone off to!"

Peter heard a combination of guilt and exuberance in his father's voice. It was always like that whenever his father had won big money.

"I know, Da. I know she's not home. She's here with us."

"Us? Who? Where is she?"

"Ma's here with me in Worcester. We're at Rayna Genrose's apartment."

"Well, by God," his father's voice boomed over the phone, "she'd better get back here straight-

MEANT TO BE

away! 'Tis good news I have. Made a bundle at the track today, a *bundle*, son, I'm tellin' you. Paid off the mortgage papers the Hawk held on me . . ."

Peter's heart fell. The old man had even mortgaged the house. No wonder he'd gone to the track despite his wife's protests. His father was still raving passionately about his winnings.

". . . I've still got plenty left over, even after settling with Hawk. Tell your ma, boyo, that we'll celebrate tonight. 'Tis a fistful of greenbacks I have—"

"Oh, Da, listen," Peter broke in, "if you love Ma like you say you do, you'll quit gambling. Rayna and I plan to get married next summer and then it'll be just you and Ma. She's had it, Da. Says she can't keep living like this, not knowing, and you're telling me that you even put up the house?" He groaned. "Ma can't take much more of that nonsense. You know that, Da."

"Oh, now lad, put your ma on the phone. Let me explain, talk to her—"

"She said no, Da, doesn't want to talk. You'd better get the bus at Park Station and come out to Worcester. When you get in, call and I'll pick you up. See if we can straighten things out with you and Ma."

He gave his father Rayna's telephone number before he hung up. He turned to Rayna.

"I know it's a horrible thought for a doctor to have, but I'd like to throttle the Hawk. I'd give anything to have that creep out of my father's life."

Ira Dohain had suggested that Maribeth stop by the state police crime lab on her way home from Baptist Hospital. The lab was in Jamaica Plain, not far from Baptist, where she finished a private-duty case involving a patient with multiple injuries from a car accident.

"I'm anxious to let you know what I've found out," he told her when he phoned.

"Right, Ira. I'll be there as soon as I get off duty."

She found the small one-story red brick building near the Arborway. Ira, dressed in a white lab coat, was alone in the brightly lit room. Laboratory equipment, beakers, banks of glass tubing, humming centrifuges, colorful flasks of various liquids on the shelves—Ira led her into the midst of this controlled confusion to a granite-topped counter in the corner of the room.

"My God, girl," he questioned, "where did you get this stuff?" The young Armenian peered at Maribeth through dark curly hair that swung across his forehead as he pointed to the small white jar on the counter.

"Know what's in this stuff?" Ira's serious tone of voice alerted Maribeth.

"Something bad?"

"Bad! More than bad, it's lethal! I've done a sample analysis and so far I believe it to be a rare form of tetrodotoxin, a toxin that affects the nervous system. Maribeth," he said in a serious voice, "in this one little white jar you've got enough poison to kill an army."

"Ohmygawd, Ira," Maribeth gasped, "you've got to be kidding me!"

"Wish I were." Ira's response was slow and measured. "Wish I were. I know you've heard of mustard gas. There's been some talk in the papers that the Germans may try to use the stuff now in the war, but, anyway, this stuff we have here is worse than mustard gas. Mustard gas is a gaseous blistering agent. But if I'm right, and I think I am, this substance is more potent than either cyanide or arsenic."

"Where does it come from? And to be so deadly? Both Mrs. D'Asardi and I handled that jar." Maribeth shuddered.

"I know. It's an ancient poison, known as far back as Egyptian times. The Chinese, the Africans . . . all the ancient civilizations have been aware of this poison."

"But how, where?" Maribeth was still confused.

"Well, it's a toxin found in the skin, liver, ovaries, and intestines of certain fish."

"What certain fish?"

"God, Maribeth, been a long time since my college biology courses, but I seem to remember something about blowfish . . . or puffers, and some species of sea toads, even mollusks and snails. Fish usually found in warm water, like the Caribbean. Many of the people in those islands use stuff like this in their voodoo practices."

"But, Ira, here in Boston? How would anyone in Boston get hold of such poison? We don't have exotic fish like puffers and sea toads . . . whatever . . . around here, do we?"

"Not that I know of, but in a port city like Boston, ships coming from all over the world, sailors, longshoremen working the docks, and don't forget with the war on, all kinds of trafficking, some . . . most of it underground. Money can buy most anything. Even a rare exotic poison."

"I guess so, Ira. I'd forgotten that a port city can be host to anything. I remember when I was a student nurse we admitted a sailor with leprosy. *That* was scary. He was shipped off to Carville, Louisiana, in a hurry."

"I know, the leprosarium. But to get back to our 'stuff' here." He indicated the material on his lab counter.

Maribeth placed her handbag and sweater on a chair and moved nearer the counter to stand beside Ira.

"Maribeth, let me tell you what I do know. I went over to the medical library and here's what I found."

He pulled out a sheaf of typed pages. "It's all here. You can take this and read about this dreadful stuff for yourself, but essentially this poison comes from a type of fish found in Japanese and Korean waters. Called a blowfish or puffer because it can swell its belly. When people eat the fish, if it's not properly prepared, it can kill."

"Are you kidding?"

"Maribeth, it's a poison very much like curare, for which there is no known antidote. A lethal dose for an adult is one to two milligrams. What you could put on the head of a pin."

Maribeth shook her head. She could scarcely believe what Ira was telling her, but he had the facts in black and white. Her legs were trembling and she sat on a stool at the lab counter, rested her chin on her hand, her elbow propped on the counter. She asked Ira because she really wanted to know the answer. "How does it kill?"

"From what I've read, Maribeth, it paralyzes the muscles. Symptoms usually appear quickly, within five to thirty minutes. Weakness, dizziness, pallor, tingling of lips and throat, increased salivation—"

"Right. When I found the patient on the steps

MEANT TO BE

there was this white froth all around his mouth," Maribeth interrupted, remembering the victim.

"That's what's indicated in this report. Also, there may be lowered blood pressure as well as body temperature, abdominal pain, muscle twitching, convulsions, that sort of thing."

"That sounds like a horrible way to die, Ira."

"This poison, Mari, is ten to a hundred times more lethal than the bite from a black widow spider and ten thousand times more deadly than cyanide."

"So, Ira, you think this salve caused Bernie Hazzard's death?"

"Sure do. Like I said, takes only a milligram or so to kill an adult. Mixed with an ointment and applied to a cut or an abrasion . . ." He raised his shoulders. "It's all you need."

Maribeth nodded, ran her tongue over her lips as she remembered seeing the bruises on Bernie's face, along with the dilated pupils of his open, staring eyes. Again she shuddered at the memory.

"Ira, it sounds horrible. Fiendish, really."

"Sure does, Maribeth, believe me."

Maribeth was thinking ahead. She had promised Ben she would not keep "meddling" in this affair, but now, with this revelation, she would have to *do* or *say* something to somebody. This could not be covered up.

She spoke up. She was anxious to hear Ira's suggestions.

"So now what do we do with this information?" she asked.

"We have got to let the police know about this. We don't want to be accused of withholding evidence in a murder case.

"Of course, Ira, you're right. The thing of it is, I promised my friend, you've met him, Ben, the police officer, that I wouldn't meddle in this mystery anymore. But you know, the more I find out the more curious I am to know what really happened to the poor young man."

"It's your nature, Maribeth. You've always wanted to know all the whys and wherefores. You can't help that."

Ira Dohain admired Maribeth for her interest and curiosity. He knew her as smart, clever, and a hard worker. In college they had done extremely well when they worked together on their assigned psych project. At first Ira knew Maribeth hadn't trusted him. Later, when they became friends, she told him how reluctant she had been to accept his friendship. "When I told Ben about this," she told him, "he said, 'Maribeth, when the hand of friendship is extended to you, accept it.'" Ira and Maribeth had been friends ever since. He had even invited Maribeth and Ben to his wedding a year ago.

Maribeth was glad that she had Ira to turn to for professional help. As a chemist at the state police laboratory he had often been called as an expert witness in criminal cases.

He fixed his dark brown eyes on Maribeth and she knew he was serious.

"I can understand your need to get at the bottom of this thing, Maribeth," he said as he waved toward the items on the counter. "I hope you don't think I'm being patronizing or presumptuous but, well, I think maybe as a colored person you feel suspect, like you're somehow involved in this problem."

"How would you know, Ira? You are not colored.

How can you know how I feel?" she asked him. She looked at his open, friendly face; then she softened her reply in a voice that indicated her reflective state. "Course you're right, Ira. I do feel as if I must clear away any suspicion the police seem to have. Oh, they haven't come right out and said anything, but I just have to find the truth. If I were a white nurse . . . well, like I said, Ira, you're not colored."

"I know I'm not of the same race as you, Maribeth, but we Armenians are people with a history much like yours. We lived through a diaspora of our own."

Maribeth studied Ira's face.

"What are you talking about, Ira? Your ancestors weren't slaves like mine, were they?" she asked, not understanding Ira's remark.

In answer, Ira shook his head, his thick dark hair curled softly around his pleasant, friendly face.

"I can understand full well your wanting to solve this mystery you seem to be involved with, Maribeth," he told her. "Like I said, your ancestors, just like mine, the Armenians, were pushed out of their country, their homeland, and . . . when something like that is part of your history, you're naturally on the defensive, always trying to prove that you are equal to anyone else."

"Right, Ira, you're right. My father always told me that no one was superior to me. Might be my equal, but definitely not better."

"Your father taught you well."

"He did. But I never knew that your countrymen were displaced."

"It's not in the history books, that's why. But my

father was only fifteen when he and my grandparents had to leave their home and all that they had."

"Awful to have something like that happen."

"It was a terrible time. My folks don't talk much about it, but the Ottoman government was determined to crush all of Armenia. In 1915 that dastardly government deported Armenian people into the desert of what we call Syria and nearly a million people died of thirst and starvation. By the grace of God my grandparents and my father got to the United States."

As Ira spoke, Maribeth could sense the deep thoughts his reflections were causing him. She understood with greater clarity his agreeing to help her in her search for the truth. She realized that her personal history, like his own, demanded validation of self-worth. She was happy that he was willing to help her. Ben, she knew, was on her side and now she had Ira Dohain. She was bound to get somewhere with this mystery.

"So, Maribeth, back to our find here..."

Ira's dark eyes were serious as he contemplated Maribeth's dilemma. He offered a suggestion.

"Why don't I do this for you? I can report to the police that you helped Mrs. D'Asardi retrieve her son's belongings from the manager, but because the 'cut salve' looked odd and had that distinct burnt-flesh odor, you asked me, as a friend, to check into it. I did and decided to report my findings to the police. They can take it from there, and I'm certain they will," he added.

"They won't be mad?"

"Don't think so. State and city police work together all the time. They might even be glad we've done the preliminary work for them. They always say we, the state police, have more money in our budget than they do in theirs."

"Thanks, Ira, for helping me out. Glad I can count on you."

"No problem, kid. Just be grateful that neither you nor Mrs. D'Asardi had any breaks in your skin when you handled the stuff or you probably wouldn't be here to thank me at all."

Maribeth knew she had to let Ben know about these latest findings. She phoned him.

"Ben!" Maribeth woke him with her frantic telephone call.

"Wha, what's up?" he answered in a sleepy voice. "Who's this? Mari—"

"Yes, Ben, it's me. I'm sorry that I woke you but I have news about that cut salve. You remember, I told you that when I took Mrs. D'Asardi to the gym I—"

"Wait, wait!" Ben's voice sounded a little clearer over the phone. "Wait, honey. I'm awake now, let me jump into the shower and I'll get right over and then you can tell me all about this news you're evidently so excited about."

"You're not going to believe it, Ben."

"I'm afraid I will, hon. Nothing surprises me anymore."

"I guarantee you this will."

"If you say so," he said. "I'll bring supper. Pizza okay?"

"Great! I'll put together a salad. See you soon, Ben."

"Ben, I'm so sorry I woke you but I could hardly wait to tell you what Ira Dohain told me about the salve."

They were putting their meal out on the coffee table: the fresh pizza that Ben brought, still hot, the salad, tomatos, cucumbers sliced with a few slices of Vidalia onions tossed in, and iced tea in tall glasses.

Maribeth talked as she served the food, handed Ben a generous helping. She served herself and grabbed the sheaf of papers that Ira had given her.

"Listen to *this*, my friend." She read aloud, "There is a Japanese fish that has such an elusive taste that people risk their lives to eat it. It's called 'Honorable fugu' in Japan. It belongs to the class *tetraodontidae* and contains in its ovaries, liver, skin, and muscles a poison known as tetrodotoxin."

She sat back watching Ben's face for a reaction.

"Well?"

"You won't be so quiet, Mr. Well, when I tell you just what this poison can do."

She took a sip of her tea and continued to read.

"A lethal dose for an adult is one to two milligrams, or enough to fit on the head of a pin. The toxin paralyzes the muscles and the victim usually dies from respiratory arrest. Symptoms usually appear within five to thirty minutes. There was a sumo wrestler who died, they said, after his third mouthful of the so-called delicacy. There can be weakness, dizziness, pallor, a feeling of doom . . . Interesting, wouldn't you say, Ben?"

He nodded, raising a slice of pizza to his mouth.

Maribeth continued to read.

"There is tingling of the lips, tongue, and throat. Muscle twitching, convulsions may appear, increased salivation. I can attest to that, Ben, because I saw that white froth all around the victim's mouth."

"Sounds like an awful way to die," Ben said.

"It really does, but there's even more. According

MEANT TO BE

to this material that Ira found and typed out for me, the neurotoxin attacks the peripheral, sheathed nerves, but does not cross the brain barrier, so the victim's mental functions are unimpaired."

"And that means . . . Don't forget, honey, my medical education is limited to first aid."

"It means, my friend, that the victim is paralyzed, but conscious, unable to speak . . . is aware of what's going on."

"And you've been messin' around with *that* stuff?" Ben shook his head despairingly.

"Well, Ira said it was a good thing we didn't handle the jar too much and that neither of us had cuts on our hands."

"I knew you were going to get into something over your head. Now what're you going to do?"

"Ira is going to meet me tomorrow and we're going to the precinct to let Captain Curry know what Ira found."

"He's got to be told, no doubt of that. And it's a good thing your friend works in a state lab that gives him reliable authority."

"I know, and I'm glad I thought to take the stuff to him. His theory is that somehow someone slipped that material into the gym and that it was used to stop the boxer's abrasions and cuts on his face. Took a while to effect him, because the trainer said, remember, 'He was rarin' to go into the eighth round.'"

"I recall him saying that. But, Maribeth, I'm concerned about you. This is not some little five-and-dime operation. Someone wanted that boxer to lose the fight! Who and why?"

* * *

The driver of the black Chrysler kept close watch on the little yellow plastic flower that bounced on the antenna of Maribeth's car. His friend said, "Follow her when she leaves the hospital. Don't let her see you. I want to know where she's living now."

So far the nurse had been at the crime lab for a little over a half hour. He was glad he had sense enough to realize that that was only a temporary stop. Now she was back in the car and driving to the South End. Funny she didn't know that her little flower was like a beacon, pointing the way for him. He had been instructed not to let her see him, not to approach the good-looking colored nurse. Just to follow and find out where she lived. He couldn't understand why his friend was interested in *her*. He could have his pick of any number of chicks in the city.

Maribeth drove into an empty space beside Jefferson Terrace House. The driver drove slowly and watched as she hurried into the large brick building. He noticed her lovely long legs that flashed provocatively beneath her white uniform as she mounted the stairs. Her reddish brown hair sparkled with fiery glints from the sun as she entered the glass doors. She was a looker all right. That's if you liked "dark meat." He'd never been interested himself, though some of the guys on the Hill always said, "The blacker the berry, the sweeter the juice." Whatever. To each his own. Well, he'd make his report. When you were from the Hill you helped a buddy out, no questions asked. Besides, he was being well paid for this little job.

* * *

MEANT TO BE

The second call came at four in the afternoon. Maribeth had slept soundly all day, was feeling refreshed and relaxed after six hours of deep sleep. She was expecting a call from Ben and was surprised when she didn't hear his deep, familiar baritone voice saying, "Hi there" when she answered the phone on its first ring.

Instead, a male voice that she could not identify spoke. "So, you couldn't leave well enough alone . . ."

"Who's this?" Maribeth demanded.

"You don't need to know," the voice reported sarcastically, "but you'd better back off. No more warnings, Miss Nurse. Stick to nursing!"

"Who are you?" Maribeth yelled into the phone.

All she heard was the hum of a dead line, nothing more.

She was more angry than frightened. From her psychiatric nursing experience at the state hospital during her training, plus her college course in psychiatry, she realized that threats were usually just threats. Untoward actions toward others were rarely talked about by the perpetrator. Usually they were just acted upon. It seemed someone was afraid of what she might uncover. She would have to be careful. What really worried her most was that now someone knew where she had relocated. That frightened her more than the telephone call. She would have to move again. Perhaps she'd be safer at her parents' home. She'd have to think that one over.

She took a shower, shampooed, and was towel-drying her hair when the phone rang again.

"Maribeth?"

"Yes."

"This is Ira. I'm glad you gave me your phone number. Bad news, I'm afraid."

"What, Ira?"

"Someone broke into the lab this noon. The toxin is gone."

Nine

"No, Ira! Gone? Where? How?" The questions tumbled from Maribeth's mouth as she listened, not believing what she'd just heard on the phone. All this on top of the anonymous call.

"It was here when I went to lunch," Ira explained, "and I know I locked the door. But when I got back, someone had jimmied the lock. You know my lab is at the end of the corridor; anyone could have gotten in. The jar was the only thing taken."

"Then somebody else knew it was there besides Mrs. D'Asardi and me. The only other person who could have known would be the person who put the salve in with Bernie's belongings."

Ira agreed. "I'd say it was someone who wanted to be sure Bernie Hazzard lost the fight, someone who bet heavily against him."

"Right." Maribeth had a sudden thought. "Ira, I'd like to go over to the gym and see Roscoe Dunlap. I'm sure he knows something."

"I don't know, Maribeth. I agree with your police officer friend, Ben. Don't think you should get mixed up in this thing. It's getting to be a serious matter."

"But don't you see, Ira? I'm already mixed up. The police think I'm somehow implicated in this, I know they do, and Ben keeps telling me the same thing that you do—leave it alone. But damn it to hell, Ira, I can't! Got to find out what happened."

"Might be better if you did back off at this point. Look, I've still got the small sample of the stuff that I tested. Why don't you and I take it to the police? And we can tell them what we do know. Do you want to do that, Maribeth?"

"Okay. I can meet you this afternoon at the precinct station. How's three o'clock?"

"Fine. I'll meet you there and we'll go in to see the captain together."

"Good. Ira?"

"Yes, Maribeth?"

"I wasn't going to say anything, but I guess I should tell you, especially if we're going to the police, but . . . I had another threatening telephone call."

"Another one?"

"Uh-huh. Didn't identify himself. Just told me to 'back off.'"

"Don't like the sound of that, Maribeth. Sounds serious. I'm like Ben now, I'm really worried about your safety. Still working nights?"

"No, taking some time off."

"Good. Maybe we can get to the bottom of this."

Captain Curry shook hands with each of them and offered them chairs in his office.

"Nice to see you again, Miss Trumbull," he said to her. Then he turned his attention to Ira.

"You say, Mr. Dohain, that you work at the state police lab?"

Ira nodded.

"You don't mind if my secretary takes notes," the captain said, indicating a female police officer seated to his left.

"Not at all," Ira said. Maribeth murmured her assent, although she noticed *she* hadn't been asked. She sensed the apparent dismissal the police captain gave her. What in hell did he think *she* was there for? It seemed to her that the white man accompanying her had more validity in the eyes of the captain than she did. Or was she becoming paranoid?

Apparently Ira understood, because he hitched his chair closer to hers, as if presenting a united front. *Good for you, Ira,* she thought, *you are a real ally.*

"*We* know, sir," Ira stated, with emphasis on the pronoun, "we know the police are investigating the death of the young man Miss Trumbull found on the hospital steps. And we know, or think we know," Ira corrected himself, "we think we know what may have caused his death."

"You do?" Captain Curry raised his eyebrows as if he didn't believe what he'd just heard.

"Indeed, sir. A rare poison called tetrodotoxin."

"Tetro what?"

"Tetrodotoxin. I brought a sample." He handed the captain a pair of rubber gloves. "You should wear these, maybe, before you touch the sample."

Ira had secured the sample tube in a double thickness of brown corrugated paper. He watched the captain unwrap it carefully to reveal the rubber-stopped glass tube that contained about half an inch of a white, waxlike substance. Ira had labeled the tube *Tetrodotoxin, taken from jar labeled "cut salve."* He had also dated the tube.

"How did you get hold of this?" the captain asked as he eyed the tube on his desk.

Ira signaled Maribeth for the answer, which she gave with hesitation.

"Mrs. D'Asardi asked me to go with her to the North End Gym to pick up her son's belongings," she said to the police captain. "Among his things was this jar labeled 'cut salve.' I guess, being a nurse, my curiosity was aroused. Wondered what was in it. So I opened it and right away noticed the burnt-flesh odor that I remembered smelling when I discovered the body. I asked Mrs. D'Asardi if I could take it to have it analyzed, that it could have a bearing on her son's death, and she said yes."

"So you took it to Ira here for analysis?"

"Yes, sir, I did."

"And you found out it contained this rare poison?"

"That's correct, sir," Ira said. "I identified it and called Miss Trumbull to tell her what I found. It's a lethal drug and should be handled with extreme caution."

"Indeed." The captain nodded toward the sealed tube lying partially exposed on his desk.

Ira continued to speak. "But I, that is, *we*, have more information. . . ."

"And that is . . ."

"The original jar containing the 'cut salve' has been stolen from my locked lab."

"Stolen, you say?" The captain's raised eyebrows showed his increased interest. "How? When?"

"Yes, sir. Today someone broke in while I was at lunch and the only thing missing is the jar labeled 'cut salve.' It's gone, and the other thing . . . Maribeth?" Ira turned again toward Maribeth.

MEANT TO BE

"I've received two telephone threats," she said to the captain.

"Threats?"

"Well, both times it was a man's voice warning me not to meddle in Bernie's death, to stick to nursing...."

"I don't like the idea of threats to you, Miss Trumbull. I heartily agree that you shouldn't be mixed up in a police investigation. Still, if you have information, as a citizen you have a duty to report what you know."

"Yes, sir," Maribeth agreed.

"I'm going to assign someone to check the lab," he told Ira. "I want to know more about the break-in. Want to check for prints. May not find much, but we need to check anyway. I'll send a forensics team over."

"Yes, sir, that will be fine. I have reported it as well, you know, to my supervisors at the lab and they're investigating."

"Good. We'll corroborate our findings."

Maribeth could hardly contain herself. She could tell by the captain's eyes, his body posture as he sat behind his desk that he had little interest in her as a viable contributor to the case. Her mind had been racing full tilt as she observed and listened to the man. Would he *forbid* her from further investigation into the boxer's murder? Did he have that authority? How did he intend to stop her? Could she be arrested? If so, for what?

She spoke up, unable to keep silent. Her churning nerves had caused a sudden dryness in her mouth, but she persevered. There had been other such times when she'd felt like this. Like that time in the operating room when the visiting surgeon had tried to intimidate her and challenge her ability. He was accustomed to having his own scrub nurse, not some student nurse. She stood up to his burlish manner and performed her tasks, passing instruments to him almost before he asked for them, and so impressed him that he not only complimented her when the procedure was completed, but informed her nursing supervisor of Maribeth's competence.

It was experiences like that that gave her the courage to challenge the police captain.

She swallowed and plunged ahead.

"You know, Captain Curry, it seems that since I found Bernie Hazzard's body on the steps of Zion Memorial Hospital, I am involved in this murder, whether I want to be or not."

She saw the captain's eyes flick wide open as he turned to face her.

"How so, miss? What makes you think that?"

"Please don't misunderstand, sir. I respect the work police do. I admire them as thoughtful, caring professionals who do their job. No matter how hazardous, how distasteful, they do it—"

"Now, Miss Trumbull," the captain interrupted.

"Let me finish, please, sir. I only want to help, not hinder. And in the back of my mind I still see the tortured faces of Rini and Salvatore D'Asardi, Bernie's parents, who want to know why their son was taken from them."

"So do we, Miss Trumbull, so do we. And that's *our* job," the captain insisted.

"I realize that, sir, but just so you know, I'm going to do all I can to help them. So, unless you legally stop me, I'm going to keep trying."

Maribeth was surprised when the captain smiled.

"Anyone ever tell you that you are stubborn, Miss Trumbull?"

"Yes, sir," Maribeth answered, "a few people have."

"Well, you are, but I want you to know, if ever I'm a patient, I want you to be my nurse. You're a fighter, and I like that. Tell you what, you keep searching for the facts, but keep this office informed. Okay? Whatever information comes to you, I want to know about it. And be careful."

"I'll do that, sir. It seems obvious to me that someone out there thinks I know something. That's why I'm getting those threatening phone calls. And more than that, someone has been following me. I relocated after the first call and the person, whoever he is, was able to find me. So I've moved back to my apartment."

"I see. Well, this does put a different slant on the situation. We'll give you protection, gladly, Miss Trumbull, and with your permission we'll monitor your incoming calls. Put on a trace—"

"Not my outgoing calls, sir. I depend on the telephone for my work," she told him.

"Certainly not."

He rose to stand behind his desk and extended his hand, indicating the meeting was over.

"Thanks for coming in, Miss Trumbull. Leave your address and telephone number with my secretary." He shook her hand.

Then he shook hands with Ira and thanked him for his information.

Ira and Maribeth left the precinct headquarters and went to Maribeth's old Chevy parked in the police parking lot.

Ira smiled as he got into the front seat beside

Maribeth, who got in behind the wheel. He patted the dashboard.

"Boy, wouldn't my wife and I like to have a car like this? Right now, though, we're both stuck with repaying our school loans and our house mortgage. Guess we're lucky we live near the T-line and can use the train." He settled his stocky body in the front seat.

"You are lucky, Ira. I don't live too close to public transportation so I'm fortunate that my dad was able to give me this old beat-up car."

Her thoughts were still on the visit they had just made. Before she turned the ignition on, she asked him, "While we're downtown, Ira, do you mind if we stop by the North End Gym? I'd like to ask Roscoe a few questions."

"Sure. I know Ben wouldn't like to have you go by yourself. Be glad to go with you."

Maribeth smiled and started the car.

"You're a real pal, Ira."

"Oh, I don't know, Maribeth. Let's just say I want to know what happened. I'm curious, too. And nothing challenges and delights me more than a mystery."

A different type of activity was going on when they reached the old building. Instead of young men boxing, punching at speed bags or body bags, there were white-uniformed painters wielding paintbrushes on the walls, carpenters on ladders working on new ceilings, electricians with snaking cables moving about the area.

Both Maribeth and Ira stood and stared in bewilderment at the confusion.

"Can I be of assistance?" a man's voice came from behind them.

"We're looking for Roscoe Dunlap," Maribeth said, turning in the direction of the voice.

"Oh, he's no longer here. Went to Florida to be near his daughter. Let me introduce myself."

Maribeth recognized the tall thin man with the dark hooded eyes as someone she had seen before.

"I'm the new owner, Harry Holtz." He shook hands with each of them.

"Sorry the place is such a mess. Have a contract with the Hirsch Brothers Razor Blade Company. They are going to sponsor the fights we plan to have here, have them broadcast live over the radio." He grinned broadly, giving his face an even more ominous look, Maribeth thought.

"Big future in the broadcast of fights, you know, 'specially now that we're winning the war. Our boys are takin' it to the Germans, eh? And the Japanese, too. Whole thing be over soon. Count on it."

Maribeth wondered how *he* could be so sure. One thing was certain. He was looking ahead to the future, preparing entertainment for the battle-weary military to come back home to in America. She recalled reading in the paper a few days earlier that housing was being developed for the men who would be returning to the sweethearts they'd left behind, eager to get married and start families. This man Harry Holtz was evidently thinking along the same lines.

Ira steered her toward the entrance, saying, "Yes, well, we can see you're very busy, Mr. Holtz. We don't want to take up too much of your time." Ira walked Maribeth toward the door, away from the chaos.

"Oh, no problem," Harry told them, smiling broadly, but with a penetrating look in his eyes.

"Come back any time. You're welcome to any of our fight cards."

When they got back into the car, Maribeth put the key in the ignition, but she did not start the motor. She looked at Ira, seated beside her.

"Ira! That's it! I mean, he's it!" Her eyes flashed knowingly.

"What are you talking about?"

"Listen, Ben and I saw that guy here the other night when we came to see Roscoe. This guy was with a pair of tough-looking goons, and Ben swore to me that they looked like underworld characters to him. I'll bet anything he's got plenty to do with Bernie Hazzard's death."

"Don't get carried away, Maribeth," Ira warned. "Talk to Ben, see what he says. After all, he's a policeman."

"You're right, Ira. But something tells me . . ."

"Careful, kid. Use your logic, not your feelings."

"That's what Ben would say."

"Okay then, talk it over with him. He'll know what to do. And you'd better touch bases with Captain Curry. I would if I were you."

Harry Holtz had recognized Maribeth. He remembered she had been with a colored guy, one that he was sure he'd seen before. He knew if he thought about it long enough, perhaps in a quiet moment he'd be able to retrieve the recollection. Harry's mind was like that. He prided himself on his ability to remember names and faces—important in his line of work. Today the colored broad was with a white guy. What was that all about? He shrugged his shoulders and walked to the corner office, once Roscoe's, now his. He was having that redecorated as well. Wanted to make a good impression on the Hirsch Brothers' fancy lawyers when they came in to complete the contracts.

Elena Malanson had been a constant source of disappointment to her parents all of her life. Not that she wasn't a lovely child, it was her strong will and stubborn behavior that gave them problems with her. Her porcelainlike, fragile beauty simply bewitched them. Plain, hardworking emigrants from Eastern Europe, they could scarcely believe that this beautiful child, with her corn-silk-blond hair, cobalt-blue eyes, and lithe, slender figure had actually been born to them.

"She's so beautiful, our Elena," Jacob told his wife more than once. "Such an angel, our daughter."

"You know, Jacob, that we spoil her," his wife remarked.

"Frannie, what's not to spoil? She's perfect, an' I want her to have whatever she wants," Elena's father insisted.

"Even if it's not good for her?" Elena's mother worried.

"It's all right," Jacob reminded her. "So what should we do . . . not give her what she wants, our only child?"

But when their daughter announced that she was going to marry Harry Holtz, her mother tried to dissuade her.

"Why, Elena, why?" she pleaded with her daughter. "Why do you want to bring such a person, a schmuck like him into our family? A nice Jewish college boy you couldn't find in all of Boston?"

Her daughter noticed the worry lines that creased her mother's forehead, but she continued to watch, unmoved, as her mother wrung her hands in desperation.

"And with your good looks, like a regular movie star, your college education . . ."

Elena still would not allow her mother's emotional state to deter her.

"Mother, Harry gives me whatever I want, so I'm going to marry him," Elena remarked, her attention on her feminine task of manicuring her nails.

She held one hand up, blew on her nails to harden the polish. "And, Mother," she said slowly as she glared at her mother, "you'd better not say anymore or we'll just go to the justice of the peace. There'll be no standing under the chuppah."

"Ah, no, no, Elena, not that! A proper wedding at temple, must be, no justice of the peace!" Her mother was horrified at the thought of a nontraditional Jewish ceremony for her only child. She gave in, said no more.

Elena Holtz kept a blind eye to her husband's business. When she met him and decided to marry him, she had determined that the less she knew about what he did, the less she would have to worry over. Her parents never knew about their son-in-law's affairs. They thought he was in the import-export business.

With her shiny, blond looks and blue eyes, the tall and slender Elena Holtz made a stunning contrast against her husband's dark, sanguineous, almost uncomely looks. They were a striking couple. They lived in a Victorian house in the suburbs.

Their only child, Harry Jr., who was their pride and joy, attended private schools. If ever he was asked about his father's business, he had been instructed to respond, "Oh, my dad's in the import-export business." He repeated the litany, "Slow now because of the war, but my dad helps supply all kinds of stuff to the government." He never had to explain. "War secrets, you understand." He'd been well coached. His personality was much like his father's. Whatever he wanted, he went after it.

Elena managed the home and kept life tranquil for her family. Her husband never brought work home and never, ever, any of his associates, with the exception of his lawyer, Marc Ogleston, a Harvard Law School graduate who was well paid to keep Harry out of legal trouble.

Elena also saw to it that her son dressed appropriately, spoke properly, and showed good manners. People were surprised by the young man's charming personality.

Elena Malanson knew it was her own willful stubbornness that had attracted her to young Harry Holtz in the first place. She realized full well that he was everything her parents did not want for their only child. She chose, however, to fall in love with a man whose lifestyle was far removed from the social strata her parents desired.

However, there was one facet of Elena's life that she kept secret. She worried and she prayed. She prayed silently at any given moment. Whenever she was alone, taking a shower, putting on makeup, having a quiet lunch, driving her car to club meetings or to her friends' homes, she prayed . . . that her son would be safe from the war and that her husband would be spared from what she knew was his criminal activity. These prayers were always on her mind, every waking hour of every day.

Harry Holtz had his mind focused on the coming meeting with the lawyers from the razor blade company. He stopped dead in his tracks as he remembered where he'd seen the colored guy that the girl had been with before in court—in uniform. He was a cop! Was the guy she was with today a cop, too? Damn it to hell, he'd have to do some checking . . . and soon.

Harry Holtz had been anxious to make a name for himself, move into an area totally under his own control. Although he had several trustworthy underlings in his employ, his only real confidant was Marc Ogleston, his longtime lawyer whose personal ambitions mirrored those of Harry's.

They had just finished a satisfying lobster dinner at one of Boston's waterfront restaurants. As usual, they were prepared to discuss business.

Harry snipped off the tip of a cigar with a small pair of scissors, lit it, and blew a few perfectly shaped smoke rings up toward the restaurant ceiling. Marc watched and waited. He knew Harry had something on his mind. After a few more puffs, Harry spoke up.

"Marc, you know what I've been thinking?"

Marc shook his head slowly. "I don't know what you've been thinking, Harry, but I know there's something on your mind."

"You're a smart guy, Marc, an' I trust you." Harry spat a bit of tobacco out of the side of his mouth before he continued, "Been keeping up with the war news?"

"Well, yes, I have." Marc knew that Harry had been restless under the mob's influence and had been eager to get out from under them with an operation of his own. He was not surprised at Harry's next remark.

"Then you know that the Allies are winning. The papers say the Soviets are making steady progress against the Germans and the Japs can't hold out much longer. So, the way I see it, our boys will be coming home soon."

"Right," Marc agreed.

"And they're going to want entertainment, excitement, something to take their minds off what they've been through."

"What are you thinking of, Harry?"

Marc watched as Harry's dark eyebrows drew close together over his hooded eyes. He could see the tension in Harry's mouth, which formed a tight line across his saturnine face. Marc recognized that Harry had been restless and introspective in their last few meetings, but at the present moment seemed slightly more relaxed as if he had made some major decisions.

He drew deeply on his cigar before he answered his lawyer.

"Sports, for one thing. Ever since you helped me get a piece of the Red Sox, I've been thinking maybe if I could get some shares of the Harlem Globetrotters' stock. And I've got my eye on a boxing arena in the North End. I think I'm going to be able to scoop it up soon."

"A boxing arena? What will you do with that?"

"See, Marc," Harry said, leaning forward, "it's my

plan to be involved in sports, all spectator sports. It's going to be the new source of cash, especially when the boys come home. They've missed it all, baseball, basketball, the fights, and even football."

"But the arena? How's that going to figure in?"

"Radio. Have the fights broadcast over the radio from the arena."

Harry sat back in his chair, picked his cigar up from the ashtray, and proceeded to relight it. He waited for Marc's response.

Marc nodded knowingly.

"It's a great idea, Harry! And especially if you can get a sponsor to advertise his product . . . you know, pay to advertise on the radio, say, such as a company that sells men's products, shaving cream, razors . . ."

"Yeah, that's the ticket! Say!" Harry snapped his fingers as the thought hit his brain. "Hirsch Brothers! They've just brought out a new safety razor. Bet they'd jump at the chance for some advertising."

Marc Ogleston placed his fingertips together in a steeple figure.

"Tell you what, Harry. You get the deed to the arena and I'll talk to the Hirsch Brothers' lawyers for a contract."

They left the restaurant soon after that, each promising the other to keep in touch.

Marc Ogleston was well aware that his client's hands were not always clean, but he took particular pains to make sure his work always remained within totally legal and lawful parameters. He knew he had a good job but he was not willing to go to jail because of any carelessness on his part.

As soon as he returned to his office he had his

secretary make an appointment with a senior partner of a law firm, attorney Morgan Francis.

Harry realized that he had two daunting tasks ahead of him. One, he would have to force Roscoe Dunlap to give up the gym. He already knew how he planned to do that, and, two, he'd have to wager a heavy bet on the guy he wanted to win the fight and secure that win with some type of insurance. He realized that Bernie Hazzard was an honest threat, a clever boxer with a terrific right-hand punch that was devastating to his opponents if he could land it. He had to have Roscoe's gym.

He had been discussing the fight one evening after dinner. He and his son, Harry Jr., home on his prep school break, were relaxing in the family room. Harry Sr. treasured these moments with his only child, who was waiting for his call-up from the air force. Harry Jr.'s wholesome good looks, dark hair, fair, clear complexion, and lively blue eyes inherited from his mother afforded young Harry a movie star handsome face like Tyrone Power or Robert Taylor. Harry loved his father. However, he wanted to be a good son and help his dad, if he could, even if it was slightly underhanded.

"So what you're telling me, Pop, is that you need something that will swing the fight in your favor in case your guy is in danger of losing?"

"Yeah, got to have some kind of insurance."

"Maybe something like knockout drops, chloral hydrate. You've heard of that, haven't you, Pop?"

"That what they're teaching you in chemistry, about knockout drops?" his father inquired, his eyebrows raised in alarm.

"No, indeed, nothing like that. But I've heard about stuff from some of the guys." Harry Jr.

reached over to take a handful of potato chips from the large bowl on the coffee table. His father shook his head benignly as he watched his son cram a handful into his mouth.

"Been a long time since I could eat like that," he said as he watched. "But, anyway," he continued, "you're not into that stuff. Doing okay in all your classes, even chemistry?"

"Never one of my best subjects, Pop, but I'm lucky my roommate, you met him when I moved in, Lee Chan, he's Chinese, and he's a whiz at chemistry—gee, he knows a lot of formulas and stuff. Boy, you know," Harry Jr. suddenly remembered, "he seems to know a lot about Chinese and foreign drugs that we don't even have here in America. I've heard him talk about strange poisons that the Chinese people take from plants, fish . . . exotic stuff that we don't have. Say, Pop, maybe Lee Chan can put something together that would slow up *your* fighter's opponent."

"Think so?"

"I could ask."

Ten

On fight night Harry the Hawk had slipped the special jar labeled *cut salve* into the hands of one of his men.

"As soon as Hazzard is cut on his face, he cuts easy, you know, see that his cut man, Johnny Prospect, gets this stuff. Make sure he uses this, damn it, not his regular stuff. Looks exactly the same, so he shouldn't notice any difference. Slip it in his cut tray. Make sure, now, and don't mess up!"

"Right, boss," his henchman said. "No problem."

When Bernie returned to his corner after the third round, he had sustained a small cut over his right eye. Johnny Prospect was aware of Bernie's tendency to bleed so he went to work immediately. He cleaned the cut, an inch-sized slice right over the eyebrow, and applied the salve. He was quite satisfied when he saw the blood coagulate immediately.

The bell rang for the start of the fourth round.

"Go get 'im, Bernie." Johnny gave Bernie an encouraging slap on the shoulder. "You kin take 'im. You're way ahead on points."

"Thanks, Johnny," Bernie mumbled through his mouthpiece as he jumped to his feet and ran across the ring. He bored into his opponent with his head and shoulders, crowding Sippowicz, making it difficult for him to defend himself.

Sippowicz stepped back onto the ropes and Bernie managed to score with a left hook that snapped his opponent's head to the left. Bernie came up with a right uppercut that pressed the other boxer closer to the ropes.

Dennis Logan grinned expectantly as he watched the fight. Bernie was going to win. His money was on the kid. He heard the crowd around him roar its approval as Bernie continued to pommel the Polish fighter, who seemed stunned by the barrage of blows that Bernie delivered to his head and midsection.

Suddenly, the young Polish fighter quickly moved to his left, out of Bernie's range. He shook his head and danced away from the battle area. Bernie followed him closely, his body bent forward, both gloves raised, protecting his face, and his eyes focused intently on the dark eyes of his foe.

The Polish lad advanced with a feint, a thrust to Bernie's head. Bernie saw his opening and threw a hard right hook that again staggered Sippowicz. But the other fighter countered with a left jab that connected with Bernie's chin and opened a small cut along his lower jaw. Bernie shook it off and again rushed his opponent to the ropes with a series of punishing body blows. Sippowicz countered with a quick hard right that landed on the left side of Bernie's face. The round ended with each man relieved to return to his own corner. The pair seemed evenly matched throughout the fight, with Bernie slightly ahead.

Johnny Prospect poured water over Bernie's head and toweled his face quickly.

"Deep breaths, Bernie!" he instructed. "Deep breaths! Suck in the air! You doin' all right! Keep crowdin' 'im so he can't get in no combos! Doin' okay, kid."

"Right," Bernie mumbled. "Water."

Johnny poured water from a bottle into Bernie's mouth, who sloshed it around vigorously before spitting it out.

Johnny worked on the cut, applying more cut salve, and he applied grease in liberal dabs to Bernie's forehead and face.

"What round?" Bernie mumbled as the mouthpiece was shoved into his mouth.

Johnny held up nine fingers before he removed the stool.

"You're okay, Bernie. Keep punchin'. You kin take 'im, you're way ahead on points."

Then the bell sounded and both fighters met in the center of the ring.

Immediately, Sippowicz delivered a stunning series of left hooks and jabs that put Bernie on the defensive. For some unknown reason Bernie's legs buckled.

Aghast, his corner shouted instructions, "Use your jab, kid! Use your jab!" But instead Bernie grabbed his opponent in an effort to stay on his feet. The crowd was screaming hysterically as Sippowicz continued to throw combinations, right crosses and left jabs, to Bernie's head and midsection. Bernie seemed momentarily defenseless against the flurries of punches.

The crowd was silent, then groaned collectively as Bernie rested his head on Sippowicz's shoulder in a tight clinch. The referee separated the fighters. At once Sippowicz came forward with a right hook that rocked Bernie. He fell, face forward, as if he'd been poleaxed. The referee moved in and started the count. Bernie rose to his feet slowly. The man in charge of the ring looked into Bernie's glazed eyes.

"You all right?" he asked.

He wiped Bernie's gloves on his shirt. Again he questioned, "All right, kid?"

Then the referee stood directly in front of Bernie. As he counted, he thrust an extended finger in front of the fighter's clouded, vacant eyes. "One, two, three." The referee's fingers pointed as he counted out the numbers. His right hand was fully opened as he continued the count with his left hand. "Six, seven, eight," he intoned.

He was not satisfied with Bernie's mumbled response. He waved both hands in the air. The fight was over.

When Dennis Logan saw Sippowicz's hand raised in victory by the referee, he broke out in a cold sweat. He had lost the house. Roscoe Dunlap, when he saw that Bernie had lost, sighed and went to his office in the far corner of the gym. He reached into his lower right-hand desk drawer and pulled out a bottle of whiskey. He poured a drink, went over to his safe, opened it, and took out a large brown envelope, which he placed on his desk beside the drink. He sat down behind the desk, swallowed the whiskey, and thought about his future. It looked bleak.

Roscoe was positive that his fighter, Bernie, would win the fight. He knew a good fighter when he saw one and he realized that Bernie Hazzard was

MEANT TO BE

one of the most gifted, natural fighters he had ever seen.

"I know you can take Sippowicz," he had confided in Bernie one night when the boxer was toweling off after a vigorous workout. "Just use your left jab to soften up his body, then a quick follow-through with a couple of right hooks to the chin. And hit him hard!" Roscoe instructed. He patted Bernie on the shoulder. "Got a lot riding on you, kid, you *gotta* win."

What Roscoe had not told Bernie was that his whole life depended on Bernie's win. He had never revealed to Bernie, or to anyone else, that the Hawk had information that could put him behind bars in the state penitentiary. Hawk could prove that Roscoe had once killed a guy. He was only eighteen at the time. It was in self-defense, but the killing had remained unsolved. Clever as usual, Harry Holtz came by the information thanks to the witness, Jimmy Crosson, who wanted money to flee to Canada to avoid the draft. The Hawk was happy to supply the funds in exchange for the information. It put Roscoe and his gym right in the Hawk's back pocket. Blackmail was the tool the Hawk used. Roscoe had paid steadily over the years for the Hawk's silence.

"You know," he had told Roscoe when he made his proposition to him, "you'll never keep this gym. If the state finds out you bumped off Yale Williams, it's the big house for you, my friend."

He watched as Roscoe's face paled with the certain knowledge that what he, Roscoe, had feared, had tried to keep hidden all these years, had finally come to light.

"Oh"—the Hawk grinned with a smile that never

reached his cold, hooded eyes—"I know it was self-defense, an' I'm not talkin', but, Rock, you know..."

Nonetheless, it was what he'd held over Roscoe's head and had steadily blackmailed him. After all these years, Roscoe felt sucked as dry as an old dog's well-chewed bone. Could he start a new life in Florida? He had his doubts. He had gambled one last time and lost. His life was over.

He was glad his beloved Becky was not alive to see his downfall. She had been so proud of him when he bought the gym and could call it his own.

"Rocky, I knew you could do it! You're my favorite *champion* forever." The best part was when she told him how proud she was to be the wife, not of just a boxer, but a trainer-manager and an owner of a real gym.

Tears filled his eyes as he remembered her and her difficult last few months dying with cancer. At least he'd had the money needed to care for her in her last days.

"Louis!" Sal D'Asardi called upstairs to his younger son.

"Yeah, Pa?" came a sleepy response.

"Got to dig p'tatas today! Come for your breakfast! Quick, we gotta start today!"

Louis pulled the covers over his head and groaned, knowing it was futile to delay. His father would only stomp up the stairs and yank him out of bed.

Resigned to his fate, but with his hatred toward his parents escalating every day that he had to work on the farm, he got up, dressed hurriedly, splashed some water on his face in the bathroom, and ran down to the kitchen where his mother served him breakfast.

"It's nice you help Papa, Louis," she said. "You're a good son. You work hard, be good, pay in the end for you, I know."

She placed a full plate of sausage and eggs in front of him, kissed the top of his curly black hair. "Papa needs you more than before with . . . with Bernie gone. You're a good boy, Louis."

If only you knew how good I really am, Louis thought as he wolfed down his breakfast.

He grabbed a straw hat hanging in the back hall. It was going to be hot as hell out there in the potato field. He raced out to the field where his father was already digging and had a whole row of the heavy brown tubers waiting for Louis to pick up and put into half-bushel baskets.

"Start puttin' inna baskets," his father instructed.

Louis grunted, started throwing the potatoes into the baskets lined up along the long rows. His mother's words echoed in his mind, *You're a good boy.* If only she knew how good he really was. Damn that nurse! She was getting too close to the truth. What could he do about her? She could ruin everything!

He shook the dirt that clung to the potatoes he'd picked up and angrily threw them into the basket.

"Easy," his father said. "Don' wanna bruise 'em. Easy."

"Okay, Pa," his son responded. That was exactly what he planned to do. Take it easy for the rest of his life. He'd show them all who Louis D'Asardi really was.

The first thing on his agenda would be the house and farm. The property had to go. His next plan was to relocate in sunny California as soon as he graduated. He would attend college at a place where the hot sun and sparkling Pacific waters welcomed its residents each and every day. For him there'd be no more early cold mornings loading a truck to take produce to the farmers' market in the city. No more backbreaking work picking beans, peas, pulling beets and carrots from the soil, and all of this before school started.

His classmates, boarders at the preparatory school he attended as a day student, started *their* day with breakfast served in the school's dining room with white tablecloths, silver service, and elegant china. Then they could walk leisurely to class. But for him, he had to drive the pickup truck to school after having made the trip to the market. A good ten miles in the opposite direction from the school. No wonder he was tense and anxious.

Well, Bernie had been taken care of already, and that morning as Louis tossed the potatoes in the basket he reminded himself that soon everything else would be settled. And in his favor. It might take time, but patience, time, and determination would see his plan work to his satisfaction, and he had plenty of all three.

Louis's untoward behavior and angry demeanor had not escaped his mother's eyes. She saw quite clearly the rebellious attitude he displayed. She mentioned it to her husband.

"Sal, Louis is changing."

"Whatta you mean changing? How?"

"He's so angry all the time. Not the nice sweet boy he used to be."

"He misses his brother, that's all!" her husband

thundered back. "It's the only way . . . he can deal with . . . with Bernie's death!"

"All right, Sal, all right," Rini conceded, but she knew her son and she knew he was angry at more than his brother's death.

Eleven

Mrs. Edson's two-family house was situated near Franklin Park. It was a municipal park, part of Boston's Emerald Necklace, a park designed by Frederick Olmsted. The neighborhood had been through several transitions with various ethnicities having lived in the area. Maribeth had learned from one of her patients that he had once lived in the very house Mrs. Edson now owned. That was before the Jewish population moved away to more affluent suburbs such as Brookline and Newton.

She finished dressing, grabbed her handbag, sweater, and keys, and went to her car in the driveway beside the house. There was a large vacant lot on the opposite side of the driveway. A chain-link fence surrounded it because an electric substation was located there. It was a warm night, Maribeth noticed, but a gentle soft breeze stirred the leaves of the tall forsythia and lilac trees that grew close to the fence. Those bushes were important to Mrs. Edson, she explained to Maribeth one day.

"My husband, Rupert, planted those bushes. 'You won't have to look at that ugly substation, my dear,' he told me when we moved in. 'Imagine,' he said, 'putting a monstrosity like that in a residential area.'"

"Your husband must have been a very thoughtful person, Mrs. Edson."

"He was, Maribeth, he really was. He was quiet, respectful, wanted me to be happy. When we bought this house we were the first colored family on the street. Back then there were mostly Jews, a few Italian and Irish families. We were a regular 'league of nations' back then."

Maribeth heard the resilience of ethnic pride in her landlady's voice.

"Changed now, though," Mrs. Edson went on. "People don't seem to have pride in how they live. Look at that mess across the street," she pointed out to Maribeth. "People keep their doors open, never clean the yard, toys and all kinds of junk outside . . ."

Maribeth knew what she meant. The three-decker across the street seemed out of place in the area of better-kept homes.

We make one step forward, Maribeth thought, thinking of the Negro pilots fighting bravely over Germany, *and then two steps backward. With the likes of trash living across the street, it's as if nobody has any pride.* She sighed, thought about the case she had for tonight, another cardiac patient.

Although it was quite warm for late spring, Maribeth remembered to carry her favorite red cardigan sweater. With it slung over her shoulders, she knew she'd be glad to have it against the early morning chill she'd feel when she left the hospital.

The very moment she put her car key in the lock she sensed she was in danger. A sort of prickling sensation in the back of her neck, a heightened awareness warned Maribeth. Before she could move, a strong, muscular arm clamped around her neck and a man's heavy hand covered her mouth. She could scarcely breathe, couldn't scream even if she wanted to. She struggled, attempted to step backward to stomp on the man's foot, but she was no match for his burly strength. She tried to claw his arms from her face and neck. He forcibly lifted her off her feet. From his mouth close to her face she could smell stale cigarette smoke when he hissed into her ear, "Quiet! Boss wants ta see ya!"

Terrified, Maribeth continued to struggle, trying to free herself, but she was half pulled, half dragged to a parked car on the street. Another man jumped out of the car. Maribeth could scarcely make out his face in the poor light from the war-dimmed street lamp. He was dressed in black, with a cap pulled down low over his eyes.

In an almost wild frenzy, Maribeth flung her head from side to side, but the two men were still able to blindfold and gag her. They tied her hands behind her back with some type of coarse rope. Hurriedly, she was pushed into the backseat of the car. She smelled stale beer, even dried vomitus, as her face was forced down onto the cracked leather seat. Only two minutes had passed since she had stepped out of the apartment to go to her hospital assignment.

Who were these men? Where were they taking her? Who was "the boss" the first one mentioned? Did this have anything to do with Bernie Hazzard's death?

Questions tumbled in Maribeth's mind. She began to take stock of her situation. She realized, in their amateur haste to kidnap her, they had not searched her or taken anything from her. She still had her car keys clenched tightly in her right hand and her pocketbook was still slung over her right shoulder. Her sweater, she figured, was probably trampled on the ground, dropped in her struggle. She did have her pair of hospital scissors and her personal stethoscope in her bag. Could she use them in any way, even if she could get at them?

One of the men spoke. "On your way to Zion Memorial, Miss Florence Nightingale?"

Maribeth mumbled against the gag, annoyed by the condescending sarcasm in his voice.

"Don' worry, 's only ten-thirty. You'll make it."

"Shut up n' drive!" the husky-voiced man admonished him.

Maribeth wondered where she was. They'd been riding only a few minutes, hadn't stopped at any traffic lights, but the road did seem to curve and twist as the car sped along. Could it be the Jamaica Way, a route she traveled from her home to the hospital? She was thrown about on the backseat as the frequent turns were negotiated.

She pressed her feet against the back of the front seat to steady herself. Her back was beginning to ache from her awkward position. Suddenly the driver took a sharp right turn and her head was thrown back against the seat. She could feel the car rumble over steel trolley tracks. Huntington Avenue? she wondered. Were they on their way to the Hill?

"Pull up here!" the kidnapper ordered the driver. "Douse the lights. Keep the motor goin', be right back!"

Maribeth heard the car door close and felt cool air on her legs as the back car door was opened.

"Okay, Miss Nurse, out!" The man yanked Maribeth from the backseat, and with his hands on her shoulders propelled her forward. She could feel cobblestones beneath her feet as she was led stumbling over the sidewalk and down a flight of stairs. A basement apartment or a cellar of some sort, she guessed.

"In here," her kidnapper directed. Maribeth half stumbled, half fell, and was pushed into a chair. This time she felt the rough cement floor beneath her rubber-soled nurse's shoes. She figured she was in a small room, because of the tone of the sound in her captor's voice, and she could feel a slight breeze from somewhere behind her. An open window, perhaps.

Husky Voice spoke again. "Okay, boss, she's here." Maribeth noticed the deferential tone in the henchman's voice and she sensed that there was another person in the room.

"Sorry to have to do this, Miss Trumbull . . ."

That voice! On my God, he knows my name, Maribeth thought.

". . . but you've been meddlin', even been to the police. I'm warnin' you to quit. You're in over your head, so you better stick to nursing and quit snoopin' around. Your folks still live in Cambridge, right?"

Maribeth thought her heartbeat could be heard by everyone in the room, it thudded so violently against her chest wall. The man was threatening her parents!

The man stopped speaking. The room was quiet, as if no one were even breathing.

Then the man added one single word in an ominous tone, "Now."

MEANT TO BE

She heard him say to her kidnapper, "Drop her off somewhere."

Despite the fact that it was a rather warm evening, Maribeth experienced a chilling shudder when Husky Voice touched her arm and led her back up the stairs to the car. Did Harry Holtz have anything to do with this?

Her kidnapper pushed her into the backseat, slammed the door, and got into the front seat.

"Boss said drop her off."

"Where?" the driver asked.

"Anywhere you like."

Ten minutes later, after they had driven around, Maribeth couldn't figure out where she was. She was let out of the car. Her hands had been untied but the mouth gag and blindfold remained in place and she was warned, "Don't take off that blindfold until you hear us go, and *remember*, the boss means business!"

When she was certain the car had gone, she untied the blindfold and the gag. She could hardly believe what she saw. The kidnappers had dropped her off across from Zion Memorial! She raced up the wide stairs, through the front door, down the corridor to the nursing office. The night supervisor looked up from her desk. It was Madeline Kauff

"Miss Trumbull, you're late," she accused. "About to assign your case to another nurse."

"I was kidnapped!"

"Kidnapped?" Then the supervisor noticed Maribeth's agitation. She saw the nurse's harried look, her rumpled white uniform, her hair tumbled wildly about her face. "Whatever are you talking about? Are you all right? You look terrible!"

Maribeth felt grateful for the other woman's concern, but she still wanted to get to her patient assignment. She picked up the pen to sign in.

"Oh no, I don't think so," the nurse supervisor said as Maribeth started to sign the registry. "We'd better call the police first about this, and you should be checked by a staff physician before you go on duty. Like I said, you do look like you've had quite an experience. Sit down and I'll call the police and send for one of the emergency room doctors."

"Thanks."

Maribeth permitted a faint smile to cross her face when Dr. Peter Logan bounced briskly into the nursing office. She was very glad to see him.

"Oh, Miss Trumbull, I understand you've just had a frightening experience. Let's have a look at you."

Maribeth smiled weakly as tears suddenly flooded her eyes. She felt her defenses start to crumble, especially when Peter Logan started to examine her. She realized that she was safe now, with caring people around her.

For his being such a large man, Maribeth was surprised by his gentle touch. His fingers were as gentle as a butterfly's wings on her face as he examined her mouth for any trauma from the gag.

"Your mouth is pretty dry, I imagine," he suggested.

Maribeth nodded in agreement.

After a few more proddings and probings, he checked her pulse and blood pressure.

"Your pulse rate is up and so is your pressure," he announced as he put his stethoscope in his coat pocket, "but that should not be unexpected, considering what you've been through. Ah," he said as two blue-coated police officers came into the room.

"You have questions, I expect, for Miss Trumbull." Peter Logan indicated to the policemen that he had completed his examination of Maribeth. He turned back to her.

"I'm leaving a prescription for a sedative for you. You're not to even *consider* going on your case tonight. See how you feel tomorrow after a good night's rest. You might even have a latent response to tonight's episode."

Not if I can help it, Maribeth thought. *They've made me more determined than ever to get to the bottom of this mystery.* The police waited until the doctor left.

They asked the usual questions: description of the car, the men, the one they called "the boss." How long was the car ride? Where did she *think* she had been taken, etc.? They finished quickly and let Maribeth know she should come down to the station and file a written complaint. She told them she would. The policemen left.

Maribeth picked up the "script" Peter Logan had written for her. She doubted that she'd need a sedative. However, it was really nice of the doctor to order one for her. She picked up her bag and prepared to leave the examining room. At the doorway she stiffened.

"Ben!"

"I've come to take you home, honey."

"How . . . how did you find out? Oh, Ben." She collapsed in his arms. The warmth and security she felt being close to him relaxed her. All at once the strength and courage she had tried to maintain melted away like winter ice in the strong sun. She started to cry now that her ordeal was over.

"How did you know?" she tried to ask him, in between her sobs.

"I've always told you that if a cop sneezes in area A, the guys down in area H will hear him and say 'Gesundheit.' You know how the scuttlebutt travels. And everyone knows I'm crazy about you, Maribeth. My lieutenant told me as soon as the radio call about you came in. Gave me the rest of the night off. This time you're going home with me!" Ben said in a no-nonsense manner.

"I . . . I—"

"No I, I's, Maribeth! I'm in charge. You're *not* going back to your place! What kind of person do you take me for? I'm making a few decisions, starting now, Miss would-be detective!"

Maribeth was ambivalent in her feeling. On one hand she was pleased that Ben was taking care of her. On the other was the nagging need to find out who was behind her kidnapping and why. But that could wait. She was happy to be with Ben and to be comforted by him.

Ben's was a typical bachelor apartment consisting of a large living room, a shiny wood floor with colorful rugs scattered about, a tiny bedroom with only a double bed and chest of drawers, and a bathroom with a tub. "Aren't you lucky?" Maribeth exclaimed when she saw the tub. "All I have is a shower in my bathroom at Mrs. Edson's. Had to make the bathroom out of a large closet," she explained.

"Well, yes, I'm glad to have a tub, and I'm going to get a bath ready for you right now."

He showed her where his little kitchen was. Maribeth was pleased with its almost surgical cleanliness.

MEANT TO BE 163

Then he went into the bedroom, pulled out a clean pair of pajamas and a cotton bathrobe.

"Here, honey, take these. I never have used them, a gift from my folks at Christmas. Under the sink in the bathroom are a pair of slippers I picked up at some hotel a while back."

He excused himself to ready her bath. Maribeth walked around the living room. It was quite attractive with soft beige walls, navy blue and white heavy drapes at the two large windows that Ben had closed the minute they walked into the apartment. She noticed several citations on the walls that focused on Ben's police career. She knew that he was a dedicated police officer with dreams and goals of his own: not only to be the best officer he could, but to rise in the ranks as high as he could. She knew that already he was studying for the lieutenant's exam.

"Bath's ready, honey. I put some bath salts in . . . really Epsom salts, to ease your aches." He smiled at Maribeth.

"Ben, I never knew you had all these citations." She pointed to the wall. "For bravery, for community work." She ticked them off. "You're much too modest."

"I *am* proud of them, but really it's my job. I love it and I try to do my best. As Negroes, you know we have to. Okay," he said with a flourish of his arms to the bathroom, "your bath awaits you, my lady."

Maribeth shook her head. "I could get used to this very easily, you know, Ben," she told him.

"Don't tell me you're on to me!" He grinned at her. "In you go!"

As Maribeth sank down into the tub of welcoming warm water, she realized that she was really glad

Ben had taken charge. Despite her stubborn nature to be independent and do for herself, there were those times when it was all right to lean on someone else, especially a good friend like Ben. Well, yes, she had to admit to herself, Ben was becoming more than a good friend. Only someone who loved her as she knew Ben did would understand that tonight she *did* need to be cared for, pampered, and surrounded by trusted security. The warm bath was perfect. Perhaps, after all, she would be able to cleanse her mind and body of the harrowing ordeal. As she lay in the warm water, a fugue of running thoughts, dark images, and memories of her tense fear raced through her mind. She could still smell the man's stale tobacco breath, the miasma of noxious odors from the repulsive stained backseat she had been forced to lie on, the henchmen's unwashed bodies that reeked from smelly perspiration and soiled clothing.

Impulsively, as if to complete her cleansing ritual, Maribeth washed and rinsed her hair, wrapped her head in a large white towel. She put on the pajamas Ben had given her. They were too large but she managed to find a safety pin to secure the bottoms around her waist. The cotton bathrobe was long and roomy; Ben was a tall man, but she felt comfortable in it.

Ben looked up at her, patted a pillow into place on the bed.

"You look very appealing, my love," he said. "Your skin is glowing, your lovely eyes are sparkling, and I'm very happy that at last you're letting me take care of you. I've wanted to, you know," he said slowly, "for a very long time."

"Yes, Ben, I know."

"Maribeth," Ben said quietly as he sat at the foot of the bed after he tucked her under the covers, "I know you went over everything with the police, but would it bother you much to go over it again—to tell me what happened? You might even think of something you didn't tell them, something that could be important."

"I don't mind at all, Ben. I'm still so mad that someone could invade my privacy, take me as a prisoner to any place they wanted. I thought this was America, or is it because I'm a female they think they can scare me!"

Ben heard the anger in Maribeth's voice and he sought to calm her.

"Don't worry, honey, they won't get away with it. Just calm down and tell me. Wait," he said.

He went into the kitchenette and returned with a tray.

"Hot chocolate and milk crackers. Now, tell me what happened."

He helped her to sit up, fluffed the pillows behind her, and listened intently as Maribeth went over her litany again. When she finished, Ben reminded her, "I'm not going to say 'I told you so,' but, honey, it's obvious to me that someone—"

"Ben," Maribeth broke in, "I think I recognized 'the boss's' voice. I think it was Harry Holtz. You remember, you got mad because I asked Ira Dohain to take me to the North End Gym? I'm sure it was his voice I heard."

"Right, I remember him. We'll start with that. Now you get to sleep. Tomorrow we'll go down to the station and file a written report. And . . . we'll let the captain know about Harry the Hawk. Now, get some sleep. I'm in the living room if you need anything." Then he kissed her.

The touch of Ben's lips on hers triggered an unbelievable response from Maribeth. Suddenly a hunger, a need she had never before experienced was awakened in her. Her arms tightened around Ben's neck and she could feel the tremors in Ben's arms as he held her close. Her need for this man overwhelmed her and she could scarcely breathe, so great was her reaction to his tenderness as he kissed her again. This time his lips were more assertive, more demanding.

Again tears fell from Maribeth's eyes as if a dam had been broken. The tension and trauma of the night's experience suddenly overwhelmed her. She sobbed as she held on to Ben. "I don't know why I'm crying so much," she apologized.

"Oh, Maribeth, sweet Jesus," he mumbled into her still damp hair that tumbled around her shoulders, "I've worried and fretted over you. I never wanted anything to happen to you . . . I've wanted to hold you for so long!" he whispered.

This time when he kissed her, Maribeth felt her heart pound, thumping so hard she was certain Ben could hear it too. She breathed deeply as if to draw Ben closer to her. To be loved, to be safe, to be secure was what she had always yearned for all of her life. Had it taken tonight's horrendous episode to prove that to her? She pushed the intruding thought out of her mind and responded to the man who held her in his arms.

Hungrily, Ben trailed white-hot kisses over Maribeth's eyes, cheeks, and neck before returning to claim her lips. His compelling energy and forcefulness as he probed her mouth with his tongue sent

MEANT TO BE

firelike waves through her body and she realized that never had she experienced such unbounded happiness.

The night's traumatic events, the personal violation she had suffered at the hands of the kidnappers, the loving care and protection Ben provided for her despite her stubborn hardheadedness, the thoughts and emotions tumbled around in Maribeth's mind and she began to cry again.

Ben stroked her face, kissed her eyes and cheeks, murmured softly to her as sobs shook her.

"You're safe, my love, and trust me, I'll see that you are always safe from now on."

"Oh, Ben, I was so scared!"

"I know, honey, I know."

It was a night neither would forget. As Maribeth lay secure in Ben's arms that night she understood with sudden clarity that although she had always thought she wanted total independence and the freedom to make her own decisions, pursue her own goals, there came a time in a woman's life, if she was lucky, when she would find her partner, the other half that made her whole.

She snuggled closer to Ben, who lay sleeping beside her. The solid warmth of his firm, muscular body assured her that she was *very* lucky. She was loved by a good man, and she loved him.

Half asleep, Ben sensed Maribeth was awake and drew her closer. He kissed her forehead and murmured, "I've waited so long to have you here beside me. Now I *know* you're safe. You're here with me, my love."

"And it's where I want to be. I love you, Ben. Guess I always have, just too hardheaded to understand . . ."

"I love you, too, my Maribeth. Have since the day I saw you at the hospital. An angel if ever I saw one," he whispered.

Maribeth answered with a kiss that led to a beginning they never wanted to end.

The next day they went to the station where they completed a written report.

"So, you think it was Harry the Hawk whose voice you heard, eh?" Captain Curry said after he reviewed Maribeth's written statement.

Maribeth nodded.

"Well, we'll get to the bottom of this situation right away. Promise you'll find out who's responsible."

"Miss Trumbull will be at my place for the next few days, sir," Ben told the captain. "If you need to reach her, that's where she'll be."

"Fine, Sergeant, good idea. Thanks for coming in, miss."

For Harry Holtz, things were working out as he had planned. It was a brilliant idea he had had when he decided to fix the fight. He had Roscoe in his pocket, made a wise bet with Dennis Logan, and very soon the gym would be his and he could start his radio broadcasting of the weekly fights with the razor blade company as a corporate sponsor. He could feel it in his bones, he was really on to something big.

Elena's folks always felt that he was not good enough for their precious Elena, but when he started making the big money, maybe take them, say, on a trip to Israel, then who would be the schmuck? All they ever talked about was going to the Holy Land. Maybe, too, he'd be able to make a substantial contribution to Zion Memorial Hospital's building fund. That would surely make him look good in their eyes. Elena's, too. No way could anyone object when he was in a business that was legit.

Twelve

A week later the detestable and regrettable business transaction (from Roscoe's point of view) between him and Harry Holtz was completed. It took only five minutes for Roscoe's life's work to be handed over to the *real* winner of the fight—Harry Holtz. Bernie Hazzard had not been the only loser in the fight with Tom Sippowicz.

In a desperate attempt to free himself from the many years of blackmailing by the Hawk, Roscoe had taken the biggest gamble of his life. He had bet his whole future, the entire North End Gym, on Bernie. If Bernie won, Harry Holtz promised to return the incriminating evidence he had been holding, evidence that indicated that Roscoe had killed one Yale Williams.

The horrendous incident that changed Roscoe's life had happened years ago on a mild summer evening. As he remembered it, he and his pal Jimmy Crosson hanging out that early evening had been looking for some excitement.

"Ya know, Jimmy, the radio's okay if you like *Amos n' Andy* or *the Shadow,*" Roscoe told his friend. Jimmy agreed. "But we got to find us some excitement. Maybe down on the avenue."

What they found changed their lives.

The seventeen-year-olds walked aimlessly down Alphonsus Street, each swigging soda pop they had spent a nickel for at Sid Sugarman's Back Bay Delicatessen.

"Here you go." Jimmy tumbled a handful of potato chips into Roscoe's outstretched hand.

"Thanks," Roscoe mumbled as he shoveled the chips into his mouth.

Roscoe felt a sudden quiver of apprehension ripple down his spine as they neared Huntington Avenue. All of his young life he'd had the uncanny ability to anticipate dire happenings. He couldn't help it. He'd feel a nervous twitch behind his left ear, or sometimes it would be a special tingling in the fingers of his right hand that would alert him to imminent danger.

Noni, his Italian grandmother on his father's side, always told him and anyone else who would listen that Roscoe had been born with special gifts.

"Jeez, Noni," he would say, trying to make light of her claims, "you're just making that stuff up!"

"Makin' up? Makin' up? When *I* saw wi' my own eyes you born wi' the caul over you face? Means anyone like you got the power to tell the future, tha' wha' it means!" she would insist. "I'm not makin' up. It's for true!"

Sure enough, tonight Roscoe sensed the familiar warning in his right hand. His palms were sweaty. He shifted the now nearly empty pop bottle under his arm to wipe his greasy wet hands on his pants.

They turned the corner onto Huntington and collided with a large colored teenager.

"Shit!" The word exploded from Jimmy's mouth as the three jockeyed for space to move.

"Wha'd you say, white boy?" The voice came from a black kid blocking their way.

Roscoe swallowed hard. He had recognized the kid, Yale Williams, so named because his mother was from Connecticut and always wanted a Yale man in her family. Roscoe had seen the young heavyweight at the North End Gym where each of them trained to learn the manly art of boxing.

"Sidewalk ain't big enough, so get the hell outta my way," Williams said in a menacing voice, his shoulders hunched up to his ears in a boxer's aggressive stance.

Roscoe bristled at the combative posture of Yale Williams. He'd be damned if he'd be a coward and back down from a spook. That would be all Jimmy'd need. It would be all over the neighborhood, "Rock chickened out," and he wouldn't be able to look anybody in the eye. Ever. He remembered the pop bottle under his arm, quickly retrieved it, grasping it by its slender neck. He advanced toward Williams.

"Hit 'im Rock!" Jimmy urged, seeing the bottle in Roscoe's upraised hand. "Hit 'im! No jigs allowed roun' 'ere!"

Jimmy Crosson, coward that he was, quickly realized that Williams was alone and that it was two against one.

Williams, however, kept moving forward.

"Goin' move outta my way, white boy?" he questioned Roscoe.

Roscoe looked at Williams and for a quick moment wished he was somewhere else. He was only a welterweight, but he had speed and quickness on his side. His trainers at the gym had always encouraged him.

MEANT TO BE   173

"Use your speed, kid. Jab n' move! You got the speed, use it!" they would tell him.

Remembering again that Jimmy was a witness to the whole scene, Roscoe knew if he backed down he'd be the laughingstock of St. Anthony's. As a boxer in training, he couldn't let it be known that he had knuckled under to a colored kid, even if the kid was bigger.

Williams threatened again. This time he pushed Roscoe back, both hands on Roscoe's chest. Jimmy was shouting for Roscoe to hit Williams. Roscoe raised the bottle over his head. He never saw the blow coming at him. Yale Williams had his right hand balled up into a tight fist. He swung up from his side and struck Roscoe on the chin. Roscoe staggered back, aware that Jimmy was behind him, yelling and shouting for him to hit back. Jimmy pushed Roscoe forward toward his opponent.

"Hit 'im, Rock! Kill the friggin' jig, Rock!"

Flustered, angered, and smarting from the blow on his chin, Roscoe ducked his head and moved in closer to Williams. With all the speed and force he could muster, Roscoe aimed the bottle directly at his opponent's open mouth. The bottle struck Williams's teeth and lower jaw. Thick glass fragments shattered all over Williams's dark face as he sputtered and clutched at his mouth. He fell back and his head hit the sidewalk with a thud.

"Come on, get up! You wanted to fight, get up!" Roscoe stood over the gasping, grunting Williams, who was trying to get up. He kept coughing, gagging, pointing to his throat.

Both Roscoe and Jimmy watched as they saw the color drain from Williams's face. Suddenly he stopped coughing, wheezed ominously, and lay still.

"He ain't getting' up, Rock. God, Rock, he ain't *movin'*! Let's get the hell outta here! Come on, move!"

"Jimmy, I didn't mean to hit 'im that hard! He was comin' at me! Ya saw that, Jimmy, didn't ya?" Roscoe breathed when they reached the safety of Jimmy's front porch.

"Jimmy, promise ya won't tell anyone was me that hit 'im! Promise!"

"Aw, jeez, Roscoe, ya hadda hit 'im! It was self-defense!"

"But what if he's dead, Jimmy! I'll end up in Charlestown State Prison!"

Roscoe's face was frozen in horror as the thought of life imprisonment crossed his mind.

"Don't worry, Rock, you're my pal n' I'd never rat on ya."

"Promise?" Roscoe pleaded.

"Promise." Jimmy Crosson's mind was racing, too. It was a promise he would quickly forget. Up on the Hill he had learned early in his young life to take advantage of every situation that presented itself. He knew there'd be no advantage to him to keep secret the information he had, not when he could get someone to pay him for it. He prided himself on being smarter than Roscoe and he knew just the person who would pay him for what he knew.

There was a small column in the *Boston Evening Courier* the next night:

PROMISING YOUNG COLORED FIGHTER FOUND DEAD
NEAR MISSION HILL

MEANT TO BE

The article stated further that the young heavyweight, promoted by Harry Holtz, had been a sure bet to win the New England Championship in the amateur heavyweight division. What the news article did not reveal was Harry the Hawk's anger at losing a boxer that he had seen as a potential winner. He'd been close to having Yale Williams turn professional and planned to groom him to enter the ranks of professional boxing. A professional heavyweight fighter meant big money and that's what the Hawk wanted.

"Ya did right, Jimmy," the Hawk told the young hoodlum who had lost no time in letting him know who was responsible for the young man's death. "Keep this info between you n' me." He smirked as he slid a fifty-dollar bill into his paid informant's hand.

Harry Holtz planned not only to have a stable of boxers, but to own a gym where boxers could be trained and an arena to accommodate two hundred or so patrons who would come to view his Friday night fight card, plus his radio boxing events with wealthy sponsors.

The incident of Yale Williams's death seemed to have been forgotten. No one was ever charged with the boxer's death. Shortly after the frightful happening, Roscoe was called into the army. Although only an infantryman, he found time to hone his skills as a boxer and became welterweight champion in his division. One of the proudest moments of his life was when he met Joe Louis, heavyweight champion of the world.

"Hear you the best fighter 'pound for pound,'" the champ told an ecstatic Roscoe.

"Yes, sir," he told the champion, "that's what they say 'bout me." He grinned happily.

Joe Louis smiled and moved on to the next well-wisher. Roscoe never forgot the moment and knew then that when the war ended and he returned to Boston he would try to make it in the fight game.

From the first, things went well. He trained daily at the North End Gym, had several successful bouts, and with the GI bill was able to purchase a three-decker house on Mission Hill. He married Becky Busnell, the girl he'd been dating since he came home from the war.

Roscoe called his wife on the phone from the gym. "Becky! Guess what?"

Patient and quiet in her manner, despite her red hair and Irish temper, his wife responded quietly. "Yes, Rock, what is it?"

"Well, know how you were saying that maybe I shouldn't keep fighting, maybe I should quit?"

"Yeah, I know. I do think you should quit," she said stoically. "It's a young man's game an' you're not exactly a young man, Rock."

"Well . . ." He drew the phrase out. "How'd you like to be the wife of the owner of the North End Gym, huh?"

"Oh, Rock, I know it's something you want, so I say yes, yes, I'd like to be such a lucky wife!"

Roscoe heard the pleasure in his wife's voice, which mirrored his own joy.

"Tell you all about it when I get home tonight," he said.

Roscoe would never forget the day Harry Holtz and two of his cohorts came into his office at the gym. It was the start of the blackmailing scheme that sucked Roscoe dry.

"Nice place," Harry remarked.

"Thanks. What can I do for you, gentlemen?"

Roscoe recognized the gangster. He tried to maintain his composure but he sensed the familiar warning in his hand.

Harry Holtz wasted no time. He took the seat that Roscoe pointed out to him, shrugged out of his camel hair coat, and proceeded to take a cigar out of a gold case. He clipped the end, rolled it around his mouth to moisten it, and one of his men sprang forward quickly to light it.

The Hawk drew a deep drag on the cigar before exhaling slowly.

"You owe me, Rock."

"Owe you? What do I owe you? I don't owe nobody, own this gym free n' clear." And in the next few minutes his life changed.

Roscoe forced himself to make eye contact with his visitor. After all, he was in his own office, on his own turf, and even though the warning tingling in his right hand made him anxious and uneasy, he vowed not to reveal his apprehension.

Harry Holtz fixed his eyes on Roscoe, much as two combatants try to stare one another down. Roscoe could see why Harry had been nicknamed the Hawk. His eyes were dark and heavy-lidded, his face thin with sallow coloring. He had an unhealthy cadaverous look. Except for his well-tailored expensive clothing and excellent grooming, in a different setting he could have been dismissed as a nobody. However, Roscoe knew instinctively that his visitor could and would change his life. Every sense, every nerve, every fiber of his body warned him.

There was a hard edge to the Hawk's voice as he continued to lock his eyes on Roscoe.

"Guess you remember some time back a colored boxer got killed up on St. Anthony's."

Roscoe released his breath, unaware that he had been holding it. So that was it! Jimmy Crosson had squealed. Roscoe had seen Jimmy only a few times after the incident. At the time things seemed the same, but now as Roscoe thought back to it, Jimmy had changed, had a distant, put-off manner. And before Roscoe enlisted into the army, Jimmy Crosson had disappeared. Word on the Hill was, "Jimmy says 'they'll have to catch me, not goin' put no uniform on me!'"

Roscoe brought his mind back to the present as the Hawk continued to speak.

"You know who I'm talkin' 'bout, Roscoe—believe you were there. In fact, you were responsible for Yale Williams's death."

"It was an accident! And it was self-defense! He hit me first, and when I hit back, he fell, hit his head on the sidewalk. That's what killed him!" Roscoe knew he was speaking too fast and too loud, but he had to make a defense for himself. It *had* been an accident.

"Oh, I know you didn't *mean* to kill my fighter. That's why you owe me. I was getting him ready for the big time, and when you killed him you took something from me!"

"I tell ya, he was bigger than me, and he hit first. . . ."

The Hawk drew the next words out slowly. "But, *you* used a weapon, a soda pop bottle. A piece of broken glass caught in his throat and that's what killed him. I have sources down at the city morgue and that's what the autopsy showed. That's manslaughter, my man, and even if you didn't

MEANT TO BE

mean to kill Williams, you are liable for voluntary manslaughter."

With that pronouncement the Hawk leaned back in his chair and puffed on his cigar as if he were celebrating a victory.

Roscoe felt clutches of fear inside his body. What was going to happen to him? Harry Holtz said Roscoe "owed" him. Suddenly, Roscoe Dunlap knew. Blackmail!

Sure enough, Harry Holtz wasted only a few more minutes.

"I have the autopsy report, as well as an eyewitness account of the whole affair, Rock," he said smoothly. "But not to worry, it's in a safe place and will stay there—depends on you." The implication in his voice did not escape Roscoe.

He got up from his chair, walked around Roscoe's office as if making an appraisal.

"Like I said before, nice place you got, Rock. You're doin' good n' I want everything to keep on goin' good for you. As long as you make the right decision, the police will just have another cold case on their hands. But remember, son, there's no statute of limitations on murder." His words chilled Roscoe to the bone. Beaten, he sat back in his chair as if to make himself a smaller target. In just a few brief moments his future had changed from hope to despair.

The transaction finally agreed upon was that if Bernie won the fight, Harry would give Roscoe all the evidence he had been holding. However, if Bernie *lost* the fight, Harry would get the deed to the North End Gym that Roscoe had worked so hard for.

"Sure, I'll even *give* you all the evidence, Rock, being as I'm a fair-minded man. You can consider your debt to me paid in full when that happens. Think that proves I'm a decent fellow, eh?" The Hawk grinned.

Roscoe didn't care anymore. His beloved Becky had died of cancer the year before. Because of one youthful indiscretion, all Roscoe owned now were the clothes on his back, a few belongings in his suitcase, and a one-way train ticket to St. Petersburg, Florida, where his only child, Amelia, lived with her husband. It was a week after the fight that Harry and his men came back to the gym to settle everything.

Harry smiled expansively when he found Roscoe waiting for him. "Well, Rock, got everything ready? I got the papers I promised you. Everythin' in here." He gave Roscoe a thick envelope. Roscoe accepted it. His eyes never strayed from the Hawk's craggy face.

"Fine, fine. Now you just sit tight for a minute, gotta get a coupla guys in here, witnesses, you know." Harry was all business.

He went to the door and called in two burly-looking young men. Dummies, Roscoe knew. The only way either of them could count to ten was on his fingers.

"Want us, boss?" one of them asked.

"Right. Want you and Al to watch me and Rock here sign some papers. Then you two gotta sign where the x's are."

"Gotcha! Whatever you say, boss."

When the signings were completed, the Hawk

MEANT TO BE

gathered all the papers and placed them in a large folder, which he put in his leather briefcase.

"I gotta give you credit, Rock, you're a man after my own heart. I like a guy like you who takes the 'ups and downs,' the 'bitter with the sweet,' so's to speak. You don't whine or beg. I like that in a man. Did good, you know. Built a right nice gym here." He smiled expansively.

Roscoe glared at his enemy. For the last time he rose slowly from behind his desk, his reluctance to move apparent. Harry Holtz saw it. Roscoe, a small, compact man, showed a certain malevolent dignity as he stood up and walked to the door. He placed his hand on the doorknob, turned, and spoke for the first time that evening.

"Forget you, Harry Holtz, to hell and back."

He stepped out and closed the door quietly. Harry couldn't help himself. He shivered. He had heard about Rock's ability to predict the future. But Harry believed in living in the present.

He shrugged his shoulders and looked around the gym with satisfaction. He could see great events taking place there. Radio broadcast contracts would be available, and he had plans for weekly fight broadcasts. He was already dickering with a potential sponsor thanks to Marc Olgeston's work with the razor blade company.

He thought about Roscoe and his *malocchio*, evil eye, and shrugged his shoulders. In life there are always winners and losers. Long ago Harry had decided to be a winner. His only small nagging worry, only unfinished business, was the jar of cut salve. He had to make certain it couldn't be traced to him or his son.

Damn, he thought, *Roscoe should never have sent the*

stuff to Bernie's mother along with her son's belongings. Admittedly, part of it was his own fault for not instructing his man to retrieve the jar once the fight was over. Good thing he'd had Dizzy follow that colored nurse or he'd never been able to trace the stuff to the state lab. It was a piece of cake to have his man break into the lab and get it. He sure hoped that kidnapping the nurse had put the fear of God into her and she'd stop snooping around.

The salve. He'd have to dispose of it and soon. He remembered how excited he'd been the day his son brought it to him.

"Pop!" the boy had called from school, "been called up! Report in ten days, the air force!"

"What?" Harry's heart dropped to his feet. Elena would be upset, but the air force was what his son wanted.

"That's great, son!" he managed to choke out, forcing cheer in his voice. "Coming home, aren't you?"

"Be home tomorrow, Pop."

His son had brought the jar of cut salve with him. He explained to his father, "I told Lee Chan, Dad, that you wanted to get rid of some wharf rats around the docks. He said if they eat any of this stuff, they will bleed, maybe their nerves and muscles will be affected, and death comes after a paralysis sets in. 'Tell your father,' he said, 'that he must wear gloves in case of any nicks or cuts on his hands when he mixes it with the rats' food.' I remember, Dad, he was really serious, said the stuff is very strong, very bad once it gets into the blood."

"That so?" Harry asked.

"Yeah, Dad. I asked him how bad and he said, 'In my country, people eat the fish this poison comes

から all the time, those that can afford it, that is. The poison is in certain parts of the stomach, liver, and other organs, but when an expert chef prepares it, it's considered a delicacy. People risk death to eat it.' Man, that's crazy. Like playing Russian roulette, I told him. 'Maybe so, but that's the way life is in the East, sometimes.' That's what Lee said."

Harry Holtz shook his head to clear away the memories of his son's report. Now his son was stationed in Ohio, learning how to fly a war plane, and his roommate, Lee Chan, had returned to his family in Hong Kong.

Harry sighed and turned his thoughts away from the disposal of the lethal salve. He'd deal with it later.

Thirteen

Ben brought dinner home that night. He had stopped by Bob the Chefs on the avenue, bought the chefs specialty, baby back ribs, peas and rice, seasoned greens and cornmeal muffins. Maribeth made a pot of coffee and they enjoyed slices of pound cake. Cold, sliced peaches completed the meal.

Maribeth was glad to see Ben. She knew that it was his solid no-nonsense approach to life that brought her comfort. Ben was quiet, never said a whole lot, but when he had something to say, his serious, thoughtful, considerate reasoning ability left no doubt in her mind this was a man she could always count on.

"Well, the captain told me that the connection with Harry Holtz was solid evidence that Holtz might be involved in Bernie Hazzard's death. You know he owns the North End Gym now."

"I know, Ben. Thought I told you that Ira Dohain and I discovered that when we went by."

"So you did. Guess I forgot." Ben smiled. "Well, anyway, the captain is looking at a blackmail theory. Roscoe Dunlap *has* disappeared and Harry Holtz is managing the fight gym now. Starting to talk about fights broadcast over the radio, Captain Curry says."

"Maybe, Ben," Maribeth said thoughtfully, "maybe there is a connection between the two, something that happened in the past."

"Could be. And," Ben added, "Captain said they've identified your kidnappers as members of the Hawk's mob."

"Really, Ben?"

"One guy's name is Al Frateoli. 'Babe' Frateoli, he's called. One of the small-time hoodlums that hang around. The 'gofer' type, IQ of seventy-five, something like that. Guess the other one is someone he picked up to help him that night."

"He was just able to follow orders without thinking of the consequences . . . like a robot."

"That's exactly the type, Maribeth. That's why I wish you'd leave this whole detecting business to the police. I worry about your being hurt. The chance of that happening is great, and, honey, you know I couldn't stand it if anything should happen to you. Understand what I'm saying?"

He put his coffee cup down on the table and reached across for Maribeth's hands. "You don't intend to make me old before my time, do you, love?"

Maribeth laughed. "I'd never do that to you, Ben."

"Well, I hope not, because you know that I love you and I intend to spend many long years with you."

Maribeth smiled coyly at him. "Ben, is that a proposal?"

"Of course." He grinned. "Will that hold you until I can get the ring?" he challenged quickly.

Maribeth leaned across the table and kissed him.

"After the other night, you just try to get away, Ben Daniels! See how far you get!"

One of the reasons Maribeth liked doing private-duty nursing at Zion Memorial was that the hospital billed the patients for nursing service and issued a check to the nurses. There was never a hassle collecting from individual patients.

She had taken a few days off after her kidnapping and had gone to pick up her last paycheck. Because it was around noon, she decided to go into the hospital cafeteria for a quick bite.

She selected a light lunch, a salad and crackers with a tall glass of tea, and found an empty table near the window. There were several workmen outside grooming the lawn of the hospital's inner courtyard, the hospital director's pride and joy. Maribeth sipped her tea as she watched the men. A man's voice intruded into her thoughts.

"Good to see you back at Zion, Miss Trumbull. How are you doing after your ordeal?"

She looked up.

"Oh, Dr. Logan, didn't see you. I'm doing fine, thanks."

"Mind if I join you?" He placed his tray on the table.

"Not at all."

"So, how are you really feeling? Doing okay?" He gave her an anxious look, as if he was examining her face for clues.

"I'm doing fine."

Peter Logan cut his sandwich into quarters. "I understand that the kidnappers might be part of Harry Holtz's gang. That right?"

MEANT TO BE

Maribeth chewed slowly and sipped more of her tea before she answered, "That's what the police think."

"I've had dealings with that character myself," Peter said slowly.

Maribeth's eyes snapped wide open at Peter's admission.

"You have?" Maribeth couldn't keep the disbelief out of her voice.

"Yes, I have. I wouldn't want it to become common knowledge here in the hospital," he sighed, "but I guess nobody really strays too far from his roots. I've been going to the North End Gym since I was a kid. That's how I got to college . . . but that's another story. Anyway, I was a pretty good amateur boxer, and every once in a while I still like to go there—great way for me to relax. Punch the speed bag, go a few rounds with a sparring partner, work up a fine body sweat, take a shower, and I'm renewed, refreshed. Clears my mind, too."

"I know what you mean. Sometimes, if I can, I like to run four, five miles," Maribeth said.

"Right. But I think you might be interested in a discovery I made the last time I was at the gym."

"Discovery?" Maribeth's eyes widened.

"Yes, Miss Trumbull." Peter Logan sighed again as if reluctant to disclose his next thoughts. "My dad is an inveterate gambler. It's not something I'm proud of, but he's been like that since I was a kid. I'm telling *you* this, but I know you'll keep my confidence. I think I've got him involved in Gamblers' Anonymous. My mother's threatened to leave him. . . ."

"That's awful. I'm sorry. I really want to know what happened to him, Doctor."

"I do too. However, I went to the gym . . . You know Harry Holtz owns it?"

"Yes, I found that out." Maribeth took another slice of tomato and chewed quietly while she waited for Peter Logan to continue.

"I was surprised when I went in and saw all the changes he had made. The place seemed brighter, even more commercial, more up-to-date. He even has a new wall safe with his picture over it. But at any rate, that day I had gone there specifically to confront Harry."

"Confront?"

"Yes, I knew my father had been gambling with him, placing wagers on fights—"

"Was he surprised to see you?" Maribeth interrupted.

"Yes. I think he was expecting some high-priced lawyers. I learned later that he intended to sign a contract with a razor blade company for weekly radio fight broadcasts. He was surprised to see me, I can tell you that. Tried to act nonchalant and casual. 'Well, well, Dr. Peter Logan! To what do we owe this visit?' he said. I was so mad I leaned over his desk and grabbed him by his necktie and pulled him to his feet. He's a tall man but really on the thin, cachectic side. I brought him to his feet so suddenly he didn't have time to alert his goons."

"What happened?"

"Well, I had my nose within an inch of his and I told him that if he *ever* made any wager, of *any* kind, with my father again, he'd have to deal with me."

"You told him that?"

"Sure did, and do you know that the son of a bitch—excuse me, Miss Trumbull, but that's what he is—do you know he defied me, challenged me?

Told me, 'Your father is a grown man and can do what he wants, *Doctor.*' Sarcastic son of a bitch!"

"What happened then?"

"He made me so mad I don't know what made me do it but I saw red! I shouldn't have done it, but I just hauled off and hit him! Knocked him on his keister. But more than that, Miss Trumbull, I'm ashamed to say now, I hit him so hard—he's craggy-faced . . . thin-faced, you know—anyway, I opened a cut right on his left cheekbone. I think my class ring caused the cut. Blood started flowing and immediately I looked for some way to stop the bleeding. That's when I saw a jar on his desk labeled 'cut salve.' I had nothing else except a clean handkerchief in my pocket, so I was going to apply pressure to the cut with that, then apply the salve. When Harry saw me reach for the jar his face turned white. He grabbed it out of my hand, screamed, 'No! No!' as if all the banshees of hell were after him, and ran out of his office to the bathroom down the corridor."

"What did you do then?"

"I went after him, asked if I could help. Told him I was sorry that I'd hit him, but that I still meant what I'd said about my father. He kept saying, 'Go away, get out of my gym and don't come back! Go away!' So I left."

"He was scared to death, Dr. Logan. He had reason to be," Maribeth said quietly. She lowered her voice. "The police know now that the cut salve is what killed Bernie. It had been mixed with a poison, tetrodotoxin, that causes nerve damage, paralysis, and death, especially if it gets into the bloodstream, like through a cut, et cetera. A friend of mine at the state lab analyzed it for me."

She watched Peter Logan's eyes widen as he began to understand the reason for Harry Holtz's strange behavior.

Peter Logan leaned back from the table. "Well, I'll be damned. That's an exotic poison found in certain puffer fish, used a lot in some religions, like voodoo, right?"

"Right." She went on to explain, "The available literature speaks of the poison, tetrodotoxin, as similar to curare. Has no known antidote."

"Wow! That's extremely interesting."

"This particular poison is twelve hundred times more lethal than cyanide. Evidently it may be found in other species of fish and plants. Used in voodoo ceremonies to create so-called zombies. From what I've read the victim becomes paralyzed but is cognizant, but because of the paralysis is unable to speak. My friend gave me a copy of the literature."

"I'd like to see it. Unbelievable. No wonder Harry freaked out."

"He had every reason to. Do you know what happened to the jar of salve?"

"No, I don't. Harry had it when he ran to the bathroom. Do you think I should let the police know it was there? I'm not too proud of my involvement, but—"

"Dr. Logan, don't involve yourself then. Call the police, perhaps you could leave an anonymous tip and tell them where to look for the jar that's been missing—at the North End Gym."

"You're right, Miss Trumbull." He got up to leave. "I'll do just that. Glad you're okay, but be careful. Oh, and another thing, Miss Trumbull, take that plastic flower off the antenna of your car.

It's like a beacon. Makes it easy for *anyone* to follow you."

Maribeth's face paled at Peter Logan's suggestion.

"Oh yes, I will. I never gave that possibility a thought." She watched the tall, red-haired man make his way out of the cafeteria. Perhaps another piece of the puzzle had dropped into place. Where could she find more answers?

She decided to visit the D'Asardis. She'd pick up some fresh vegetables, fresh blueberries, take some to her parents in Cambridge. Her mother could make her father's favorite blueberry pie.

"No cheese for your meat sauce and pasta, Louis?"

"No, thanks, Mama."

"What's wrong? You always like plenty cheese." She threw a worried look at him. "You sick?"

"Just don't want it tonight, Ma," her son insisted as Rini D'Asardi handed him the jar of grated cheese.

"But I don' understand, pasta's no good without cheese."

"I said no, thanks!" Louis insisted, his voice slightly raised as he rejected the jar she offered him.

"So, stop arguing, pass it over!" Sal D'Asardi directed. "If he don' wan' it, he don' wan' it. Bernie"—his voice choked and his eyes filled with tears—"he always liked plenty Parmesan on his meat sauce."

At the mention of his dead son, his wife drew in a quick sob—her hands to her mouth as if to stifle it. She saw the pain in her husband's face and it upset her. Their son, however, watched with satisfaction as his father sprinkled a generous amount of the grated cheese on his meat sauce and spaghetti.

"More wine, Rini," Sal said to his wife.

"Yes, Sal, right away."

She retrieved a full bottle of Chianti wine from the sideboard and refilled her husband's glass. He smiled at her and squeezed her hand affectionately. "Thanks, Rini." Then he turned his attention to his son.

"Tomorrow, when you come from school, pick the rest of the ripe tomatoes. The crop is passin' by, but I can still get a good price. People like my beefsteak tomatoes," he said proudly.

"Yes, Pa," Louis answered. He looked at his mother, who sprinkled grated cheese on her food.

She saw his glance and misinterpreted it. "You want more pasta, Louis?" She started to rise from her seat to go into the kitchen for more food, but he stayed her with a hand gesture.

"No, Ma, I'm not too hungry. Got to study for exams. Big tests in school tomorrow."

"Good, son, you study hard," she told him. With a warm smile, she added, "You make us proud, your father and me."

Her son asked to be excused and left. His father watched him leave—shook his head, reached for the wine bottle.

"Sal," Rini pleaded to her husband, "don't drink so much wine. You know the doctor—"

"Rini, Rini." He continued to shake his head in dismay. The candelabra over the table reflected the silver glints in his dark hair. His wife saw the harsh worry lines that had etched themselves in his swarthy face. He was still handsome to her. She loved him deeply and wished that she could offer him a feeling of peace. Since Bernie's death her husband had become bitter.

"Rini, I *have* to drink. My firstborn son is dead and my youngest hates me."

"No, Sal, no! Don't say such a thing. Maybe he doesn't like farming—doesn't mean he hates you. Don't think such a thing of your own child." She rose from her seat at the end of the table and moved to his side. Suddenly, as if struck, she gasped for air and clutched at her abdomen. "Oh, oh," she moaned weakly.

"What, what's wrong, Rini?" her husband asked.

She grabbed her head as she stumbled into her husband's arms. He reached for her before she almost fell.

"My head is splitting, Sal. I ache all over. I . . . oh, my head . . ."

Sal carried his wife into the living room. Her head hung limply against his shoulder. Her eyes closed, she continued to moan in obvious pain. "My head, my stomach." Her speech was slurred and Sal could hardly understand what she was attempting to say.

He shouted for Louis to help him.

"Louis, Louis! Come quick! Your mama is sick! Come here!" He saw his wife's face flush a deep red, her eyes were wide open, shiny, moist, and a frothy fluid oozed out of her open mouth.

"Oh, Rini, Rini, what's the matter?"

A sudden abdominal cramp seized him and he fell to his knees on the floor. The pain was intense. Then he felt his heart begin to race with such speed that he gasped for air. His face was drenched with perspiration, he felt an enveloping chill all over his body. *Oh God,* he thought, *I'm dying.* He tried to say the Act of Contrition that he had learned as a child, but the frothy saliva that filled his mouth almost choked him. He could not swallow. His throat muscles were paralyzed. His pupils dilated wide and all he could see was his wife, Rini. She was very quiet. He fell over her body and was still.

Louis D'Asardi had set his alarm clock to five in the morning. As soon as it went off he got up and went downstairs to the living room. He proceeded to drag his dead parents down to the cellar. First his father, a stocky, well-built man, so Louis had to drag him off of his mother's dead body by the heels, bumping the dead man's head down the wooden stairs to the cellar and along the cement floor to the coal bin. The day before he had waited until his parents had left for their weekly shopping trip, which usually took most of the afternoon, and he had fashioned a slight trench in the coal pile. Then he laid a tarpaulin across the trench.

After settling his father's body in the tarpaulin-lined trench, he returned upstairs for his mother. She was small and slender so he had no difficulty picking her up in his arms and taking her body to the cellar. He placed his mother's body on top of her husband's, wrapped the tarpaulin over them, thinking lewdly that it was the first time his mother was on top. He shoveled coal over them until he was satisfied that they were well hidden; then he returned upstairs.

He washed the dishes that had been left from the

previous evening's meal. He dumped the uneaten food into a container that he took out to a compost pile in the woods behind the house. He distributed the food leavings throughout the composting material; then he washed the shovel he had used.

When he went back into the living room he turned over tables, lamps, chairs, threw cushions and pillows about. He would say when questioned that a burglar/murderer had entered the house while he was at school.

After he had ransacked the room he returned to his room to shower and get ready for school. He dressed quickly—putting on a pair of gray slacks and his Crofton Hall varsity sweater he had earned playing baseball. It was getting late. He had missed the first two periods, study hall and French. He'd make up an excuse, one that his teacher would accept. He had very few absences so it wouldn't be difficult for him.

He picked up the keys to his father's pickup truck and went to the front door. When he placed his hand on the doorknob to leave, he saw a car come into the front circular drive. Damn, it was that busybody colored nurse. He'd have to get rid of her—and soon!

Everything had gone just as he'd planned. He would not allow this woman to get in his way. He had always prided himself as a quick thinker. Today was no exception. Thank God he had saved some of the stuff. It was readily available, but hopefully this would be the last time he'd have to use it. He'd let Miss Nosy Nurse in, act normal, and do what he had to do. He watched her get out of the car and approach the house. He smiled broadly as he opened the door.

Fourteen

Maribeth thought about Ben Daniels. How important this stalwart, quiet man had become in her life. He'd be upset, she knew, if she'd told him she wanted to visit the D'Asardis once more. But to Maribeth it was like closing a chapter, completing a task she had set out to do. Certainly Ben would understand that and not be upset with her.

She felt rewarded, good about herself and the accomplishments she'd been able to make. She had a good education, a satisfying profession with the promise of someday being a professor in nursing, her own apartment, and even though it was old, her own car. And best of all, she realized, was her loving relationship with Ben. Each felt the future for them was safe and secure. They loved each other.

She was almost certain that Harry Holtz was somehow involved in Bernie Hazzard's death. She knew there was nothing she could tell the D'Asardis today except that the police were working diligently to solve the murder of their eldest son, and now everyone seemed to know it was murder.

She drove into the circular driveway in front of the D'Asardi house. At once she was shocked by what she saw. She sat, unmoving, in the car, not be-

MEANT TO BE

lieving her eyes. What had happened? Instead of colorful rows of fresh vegetables arranged enticingly on the shelves and counters of the roadside stand, there were empty bins, wooden produce boxes lying about, dried, browning ears of corn, flies buzzing over rotting tomatoes. And the red and green peppers, instead of being arrayed in glistening rows like jewels, were wrinkled, shriveled up, and spoiling. Maribeth could not believe what she saw, but it had been a hot, sunny day, and it didn't take vegetables long to spoil in hot weather. Something was very wrong.

Slowly, hesitantly, she got out of her car and walked the short distance to the front door. It opened before she could knock. She gasped, her hand to her chest.

She hardly recognized young Louis D'Asardi. His dark eyes were wide, as if he couldn't take in all that he wanted to see. His hair was in wild disarray and his gray slacks and varsity sweater with CROFTON HALL on it were dirty.

"Louis!" Maribeth blurted out. "Is everything all right? Your folks . . ."

"Yes, yes, they're here. Come in, Miss Trumbull. Come in." He stepped aside to allow her to step inside. Maribeth hesitated for a split second. Louis smiled at her and for a brief moment looked more like the young man she had met weeks ago, it seemed to her now.

"I didn't know you went to Crofton," she said as she stepped into the living room.

"Yeah, day student, senior year," he answered laconically. Then he smiled again. A cold feeling swept over her.

In the back of Maribeth's mind a troubling

thought pushed itself forward. Despite the bright summer day, a sudden chill flowed over her as if a door had been opened to let in a cool breeze.

What she saw then distressed her even more. It was the same untidy duplication of what she'd seen outside. The comfortable, attractive, bright living room that had so entranced her before was a total mass of confusion, of chaos. Tables, lamps had been overturned, chairs upended, cushions tossed about. The place looked as if someone has been on a furious rampage. Louis D'Asardi flicked another smile at Maribeth, straightened a chair, and offered her a seat. He gave no explanation for the condition of the room.

"I'll get my mother," he said. When he moved past her, the air stirred slightly and Maribeth noticed the distinct odor of burnt flesh. Her heart fell. What had she stumbled into? Worse still, no one knew she had planned this visit. Big mistake, she realized. She should have told someone. Why hadn't she listened to Ben? Now she was in real trouble.

The note was on Captain Curry's desk when he returned to his office after his administrative meeting.

Call from Zion Memorial Hospital. A Dr. Peter Logan says evidence re Bernie Hazzard's murder can be located at the North End Gym. Check out the Hawk. The message had been received at ten A.M.

Captain Curry read the note, stuck it on his outspindle, and summoned two officers assigned to him. He decided to follow this lead himself.

"Need to go to the North End Gym." He briefed them on the case. "Pick up a search and seizure warrant from Judge Hawkins. The evidence we're looking for may be there." He told them about the jar of cut salve. "Harry Holtz, the mobster, may be on the premises. He may possibly be an accessory to murder. If you find the stuff, inform this office and we'll get a bench warrant for his arrest. No bubble and siren now, just routine investigation. If we need the 'paper' for Harry Holtz, I'll send it by another blue and white. Harry's a small-time mob operator, but he could be trouble. From what I know of his history, he doesn't usually carry but that doesn't mean his men won't be armed."

Harry was expecting visitors that morning, the lawyers from the Hirsch Brothers Razor Blade Company. He was ready. He'd even laid in a supply of Cuban cigars for a victory smoke and he had chilled wine in his small refrigerator.

Two well-dressed men came into Harry's office about ten-thirty. They were ushered in by one of his men.

"Anything you need, Mr. Holtz, sir?" his major henchman, Frank, inquired.

"No, thanks, Frank. Come in, gentlemen, come in."

Harry was effusive in his greeting, bounding from behind his desk to shake the visitors' hands. Each man was well dressed in a dark business suit, wore dark brown cordovan leather shoes, and looked very successful. The older one, evidently the team leader, wore black-rimmed glasses that gave him a professional look.

"Can I get you gentlemen anything? Coffee, a

drink?" Harry offered, anxious to start on a favorable note.

The response was quick and decisive from the senior lawyers.

"No, thanks, Mr. Holtz. I'm Morgan Francis, of Francis, Gefford and Lessard. Here's my card." He handed Harry an impressive embossed business card, which he had taken from a leather card folder. Harry noticed the man did not offer to shake hands. Harry gritted his teeth at the obvious slight.

"This is Mr. Anglin, a junior partner in our firm." Morgan Francis indicated the well-dressed young man who had accompanied him. "I'd like to get to the business at hand. I presume you have the necessary papers and documents for this transaction?"

"Yes, sir, everything! Everything is here in the wall safe. When I remodeled the place I had a new one installed behind the picture here."

Harry was not aware of the look of distaste on the older lawyer's face. Francis did not like dealing with men with Harry's reputation and background. But he had a job to do, so he sighed and watched Harry move aside a rather formal picture of himself that covered the wall safe. He turned the dials, reached in, and removed a large brown envelope. Harry pushed aside a small white jar, frowned. *Damn, should have gotten rid of this stiff.* His problem was his ambivalence about it. He hadn't figured out how to dispose of the deadly material safely, and on the other hand he wondered if he might need it some day. He closed the safe door partially and turned to face the two men who sat on the opposite side of his desk. He'd gone over everything with his lawyer,

Marc Ogleston, and today's business was simple, merely signing the agreements.

The lawyers kept their eyes on Harry, watched as he nervously removed the papers from the envelope to place them on the desk in front of him. The other lawyer had just reached for the papers to look them over when the door opened. Two uniformed police officers came into the room, flashing their badges.

"Police! I'm Officer Shelbourne," one of them announced.

Harry's henchman, Frank, hovered at the door, distinctly disturbed that he hadn't been able to prevent the police from entering. "Couldn't stop 'em, boss," he lamented, wringing his hands. "They got papers..."

"What's this all about, Officer?" Harry stood up quickly. "What right do you have to come into my office like this?"

"We have a warrant to search and seize any material or evidence that you may have here in connection with the death of Bernie Hazzard."

Harry sat down abruptly. "Call my lawyer."

"No need of that, sir. You haven't been charged with anything, yet," the officer said.

Morgan Francis spoke quickly. "Officer Shelbourne, is it?" He extended his hand to shake the policeman's hand, a gesture that further grated on Harry's already tingling nerves. The police officer turned his attention to him. This was not what he had planned.

"I'm Morgan Francis. Here's my card. We were here to conclude a business transaction with Mr. Holtz, but your concern surely takes precedence over ours. So, with your permission, sir, we'll leave.

As you can see by our cards, we represent the Hirsch Brothers Razor Blade Company. If you have any questions, you know where to reach us."

Openmouthed, Harry watched the men pick up their briefcases and leave. Deep in his heart he knew his plans were falling apart. Angry at the police for their intrusion, he tried desperately to put on a show of power—of his knowledge of the legal system.

"I'll have your badges for this, you bastards," he scoffed at them as they methodically went about the search. "You're invading my privacy and under the Constitution of the United States that's against the law!"

A policeman was checking bookcases, drawers, various file cabinets in the room while Harry Holtz continued to protest.

Officer Shelbourne answered quickly, "Not with this piece of paper, search and seizure warrant, that tells me I can search behind walls, pull up every floorboard, dismantle every piece of furniture in this room, even the light fixtures. But . . ." Officer Shelbourne stood in front of the open safe. "Hello, what have we here?" He looked into the safe. He pulled rubber gloves from his pocket and put them on. He reached into the safe, picked up the jar of cut salve, and dropped it into a brown evidence bag, sealed it, and identified it with a label.

Harry watched as the evidence against him was gathered.

"Don't know anything about that!" he said defiantly. "Roscoe must have left it when he sold me the place. Don't know a thing about the stuff."

The police officer looked at Harry and grinned. "Oh, Harry, Harry, I've been to this gym hundreds of times. Roscoe Dunlap had the neatest, cutest little floor safe you'd ever want to see. This is a new one, Harry. Shame on you, trying to trick me like that! Tsk, tsk. Say, Harry, mind if I use your phone?" He picked up the phone and dialed headquarters.

"Yes, Captain. We found it. Okay, will do."

Officer Shelbourne put down the telephone and instructed his colleague, "Cuff 'im, Jack." To Harry he said, "Warrant's on the way. Conspiracy to commit murder. You're going downtown with us."

Harry Holtz turned pale and slumped in his chair.

Maribeth noted a strange look come over Louis D'Asardi as he came back into the living room.

"My mother says it'll be a while before she can see you."

Maribeth felt quick relief. She stood up to leave. "Well, I'll go then, Louis. I don't want to disturb her if she's busy." As she did so, the teenager stepped toward her.

"Sit down, Miss Trumbull." Then his voice softened. "You asked me about Crofton Hall. I've been taught to answer questions. So while we wait for my mother, let me tell you, about Crofton Hall, that is."

Maribeth knew that she was alone in the presence of a very sick young man and she was scared more than ever.

He started to speak in a rambling monotone. His eyes were not as wild looking as before and he seemed detached from his surroundings, as if he did not notice the chaos.

"You know," he said, "Bernie didn't get to go to

Crofton like I did. Didn't really have the brains for it. So it's just as well, no money was wasted on him. I'd have hated that, you know, spending money on Bernie would have been a big waste. Anyway, the folks could see that since *I* had the potential, the brains, I always wanted to be an architect, I could go as a day student, a 'townie.'"

Maribeth noticed a sardonic twist now in Louis's smile as he continued. Maribeth felt ice water in her veins, and her stomach churned with nerves, but she dared not show fear. She willed herself to put a calm, interested look on her face as she listened to the young man's crazy, sick narrative.

"It does something to you, Miss Trumbull, when you realize that as a townie you're looked down on. I always wanted to be a boarder, live on campus like Harry Holtz and Lee Chan. My father had the money and could have let me live on campus like the others, but no, he was too cheap." Louis fairly spat the last words out of his mouth. His eyes narrowed in contempt when he said his father was too cheap.

"Harry Holtz's father, everybody at school knew, was a mobster. Course he gave scads of money to the school, so *he* bought his way in, and Lee Chan's father, a Chinaman from Hong Kong, he gave Crofton Hall money, too, but not *my* father! He was tight with his money. 'Might need it for the farm, new tools, new parts for the tractor. With the war on, you can't even get parts,'" he mimicked his father. "So, anyway, I had to be a townie. And besides that, work every minute on this damn farm when I was not in school! I hated it, knew soon as I could I would split. Leave this damn farm. I hate it! Anyway, Bernie, being older, could get away. He had

MEANT TO BE

boxing, you know. Bernie was all right. We were never close, he's a half brother. My father had him by his first wife. She died and my father married Mother and then they had me. So, Bernie doesn't count, not to me, anyway. Course I didn't know they, Harry's father, that is, planned to kill him. But that turned out to be okay because it meant I didn't have to," he rambled on. "Harry Holtz did me a favor." His explanation was cold, matter-of-fact.

Maribeth froze in her chair. Louis was telling her that he had wanted his brother dead. God, how could she get away from him? Why had she come to this farm? Why hadn't she told someone where she was going?

She made herself take a deep breath before she plunged ahead and interrupted Louis. She was afraid to hear the rest, whatever it was.

"Louis," she said, hoping her voice sounded normal, "I can't stay much longer. I have to get back, just came to see your folks, buy fresh vegetables. I have to get to the hospital."

Louis's eyes narrowed and he leaned forward in his chair, his knees almost touching hers. Maribeth couldn't help herself. She shrank back into her seat.

"You're not going anywhere, Miss Trumbull, until I'm finished with my story. I know you came here to satisfy your curiosity. So, please, don't interrupt me again. Please. I don't want to hurt you." Again he smiled.

Maribeth felt as if a sheet of ice had pressed itself against her back. She knew if she didn't control herself she would start to shiver from the abject fear that had come over her. In psychology class, she remembered, she had been taught to "hold on to reality" in dealing with a psychotic person. It was all she could do now. She sighed, leaned back in her chair as if relaxed.

"Please. I'm sorry, Louis," she forced herself to say. "Please go on with your story."

"Yes, now, that's better," he answered calmly. "Like I said, I didn't see why I couldn't be like Harry and Lee. They weren't any *better* than I was, neither one as good, really—wanted to be a live-in student at least in my *senior* year. The three of us were teammates in chemistry. I wasn't bad in chemistry, could hold my own. Harry was barely passing, but Lee was a chemistry whiz. Anyway, I heard Harry say something about finding a poison to get rid of rats around the waterfront. He said that his dad had some rental property there. That's when Lee mentioned a toxin found in certain fish in the Orient. Said if he could get to a Chinese restaurant he could probably get the stuff. I told them my father sold a lot of fresh vegetables in Chinatown and I could take them to the merchants to get whatever they needed. So that's what we did. Chan got hold of some special dried-up powder from some Chinese cook. Dried puffer fish, I think he said. He explained that the stuff was lethal. I didn't know until later that Harry's father intended to use it on Bernie to queer the fight, but after Bernie died, I was just as pleased. Don't know why he wanted Bernie dead, really—"

"You . . . were pleased?" Maribeth interrupted, hardly believing what she'd heard.

"Of course. That meant that *everything* would be all mine, the house, the farm, all the money. Could do whatever I wanted. Be a real student at Crofton Hall, not some poor Dago kid, when I *knew* I was bet-

ter than most of the kids there. I could have my own car like the other rich kids. I could have it all. Do you know, Miss Trumbull, the first thing I did?"

Maribeth shook her head, afraid to speak.

"I went back to the chem lab at school the next day, found some more of that powder, and mixed up some more stuff, just in case . . ."

"In case?"

"In case I should need more. You know that Harry was called up to join the air force, and Lee went home to Hong Kong. All that was left for me was life on this friggin' farm. Excuse my language, but that's all I had. Except for *my* mix of tetrodotoxin. I still have some left, Miss Trumbull. The folks didn't need much. I mixed it in the salad dressing. You know Italians eat a lot of salad. You like salads, Miss Trumbull? Me, I was never a salad eater. Always like my vegetables cooked. My mother knew that. Oh my goodness." He widened his eyes. "My mother would be very upset if I don't offer you something." He got up from his chair. "Coffee and anisette cookies be all right?" His grin scared Maribeth. He was talking about his parents in the past tense.

Maribeth realized then that this crazy young man had already killed his parents. He probably hadn't wanted them to learn of his involvement in Bernie's death. This suspicious, paranoid, physically strong young man was dangerous. He was sick, possessed by what she'd heard called "murderous envy," an evil envy of those who had more than he thought he had. She had to get away from him. But how? She'd have to go along with him as if things were normal. She needed time.

"I did enjoy your mother's cookies, Louis, and coffee does sound good."

"I'll go and get some coffee and cookies, too." He started to leave, turned to her. He smiled. Chills ran down her back when she saw his sardonic smile. "Don't try to leave, I've already locked the front door and I'm locking this one when I go to the kitchen. Be right back," he said cheerfully, as if she needn't worry. Sure enough, Maribeth heard the key turn in the lock.

She jumped up the minute he left the room. She checked the windows. They had been secured with window screws that could only be opened with a key. The door to the front hall was locked, as Louis had said. Panicked now, Maribeth swung around to check the French doors that led to the terrace. They, too, had been locked with special screws. She was trapped. She leaned her head forward on the cool glass and thought she saw a dark shadow in the far corner of the terrace near the wall of the house. She scurried back to her chair as she heard the key in the door and Louis entered, carrying a tray with the same delicate cups that his mother had used before, and a carafe of coffee. Was there poison in the coffee, in the cookies?

She accepted the coffee and tried to keep her hands from shaking. She raised it to her lips to take a sip. She saw the triumphant look in her host's eyes as he raised his cup to her in a cheerful gesture.

"Cheers, Miss Trumbull."

"Cheers, Louis," she responded.

Fifteen

At the sound of breaking glass, Maribeth turned her head in time to see two Boston police officers crash through the French doors. She screamed, dropped the cup she had been holding, and ran for safety to crouch behind a broken chair. Shards of glass, splintered wooden frames littered the floor of the already ransacked room. Maribeth watched as the men moved toward Louis, their guns trained on him.

She clamped her hands over her mouth to stifle the screams erupting from her throat. Her stomach churned with roiling nerves—her breath came in gasps. Wide-eyed, she saw that Louis stood silently, his cup still raised to his lips as if he were at a formal garden party.

"Stop, don't let him drink that!" she yelled. With alert understanding, one officer knocked the cup to the floor.

"On the floor! On your belly, hands behind your head!" he barked. He handcuffed Louis and led him outside to a squad car while Maribeth watched, trembling from her near brush with death.

The other officer approached Maribeth. "Are you all right, Miss Trumbull?"

Still trembling, she mumbled, "Yes . . . yes . . . I

am, thanks." She pointed to the smashed cup. "Could be poison."

"Don't worry, we'll secure the scene. You'd better sit down." He led her to the couch. "Sit here for a moment, I'll be back." She saw him put on rubber gloves, then gather the broken cup and place it in a paper bag.

Maribeth told Ben later that what people always said was true. "Ben, my whole life flew across my mind in the few seconds between the time I put the cup to my lips and the police broke through those French doors. I just knew I was going to die."

"Sorry, Mari, that you had to go through such an ordeal. Must have been awful." They were at Ben's apartment, talking about the incident that had nearly cost Maribeth her life.

"It was. How did the police know where I was?"

"They got a tip from Dr. Logan that there was evidence at the North End Gym."

Maribeth's eyes widened. "Then Peter Logan *did* make the call," she murmured. "I thought he would."

"Yes, well, the captain said that was all they needed, honey, to go and question Harry."

Maribeth sighed deeply. It had been a most eventful day. Seeing the D'Asardi home in such unlikely chaos and upheaval, forcing herself to look at her own death in the face of Louis D'Asardi, having the police rescue her when she despaired of all hope, writing out and signing the many forms required by the police—it had been horrible.

"So," Maribeth said as she sat close to Ben on the couch in his living room, "so, really, Harry Holtz was the one who sent them to the D'Asardi farm."

Ben pulled Maribeth even closer before he spoke. The thought that Maribeth might have been killed by the raving, ranting, unstable young Louis D'Asardi was almost too real to comprehend. He ran his hand up and down her arm as if to reassure himself that she was really sitting beside him.

"From what I hear, the police know that Harry had been blackmailing Roscoe for years. The talk is that Harry had proof that Roscoe had killed a guy years back. He threatened to tell. So Rock bet on Bernie. If Bernie won, Harry promised to give Rock the 'papers' he held on him. So Harry, determined to get the North End Gym, fixed it so Bernie would lose. I don't believe he meant to kill the boxer, only to slow him down so he would lose the fight."

"Why didn't Roscoe sell the place to Harry?"

"The word I got was that the gym was his pride and joy. It was his life, honey. Meant a lot to him, and besides, Harry was bleeding him dry, had been blackmailing him about the manslaughter charge and Roscoe wanted it to stop."

"How did Roscoe make out in Florida?"

"He didn't. Things were bad for him when his wife died, but when he lost the gym . . ."

"The straw that broke the camel's back," Maribeth contributed.

"You could say that, sweetheart. His daughter told his friends that he didn't seem to care about anything. Understand he died last month."

"Poor Roscoe," Maribeth murmured.

"I know . . . after going through the war an' all. They did give him a military funeral, though," Ben volunteered.

"He'd have been proud of that. I always thought

he was a decent human being, Ben. It was too bad that things happened the way they did."

Ben continued to tell Maribeth about the police activity at the gym.

"When the police found the jar of cut salve in Harry's safe, they arrested him. The charge is conspiracy to commit murder. Like I just said, I don't think Harry planned on killing the boxer . . . just wanted to slow him down enough so *his* fighter would win. But you know 'conspiracy to commit murder' carries the same penalty as murder."

"Oh my God, I didn't know that."

"Yep, and once he, Holtz, was arrested he tried to cut a deal, told the police that they might find something at the D'Asardi farm. He was anxious to keep his son out of the picture if he could. He knew the D'Asardi boy and the Chinese lad were involved in securing the poison."

Ben absentmindedly stroked Maribeth's arm as he pulled her close. She rested her head on his shoulder and listened to his story. She shivered involuntarily as Ben began to fill her in on what he had learned.

"The crime scene, the whole house, really, was secured and the crime scene investigators began their search."

"Where did they find the D'Asardis?"

"Said it was easy. All they had to do was follow the trail of scuff marks where the kid had evidently dragged his father's body down the stairs, across the cellar floor, to the coal bin. They both were there, under the coal, wrapped in a tarpaulin."

"Ben, they were very nice people. They deserved better than that." She shook her head.

"I'm sure they did their best, what they thought

was right for their family, but you just never know," Ben said.

"Tell me about it. Today scientists are talking about DNA, genetic markers, and you never know what composite of markers you've been given."

"Oh yes, Mari, something else. The police found the powder in the kitchen, hidden on a back shelf . . . some kind of Chinese writing on it. And the medical examiner has decided death was respiratory paralysis. Found the poison in the blood of both."

"Ben, I think he had put some of that powder in my coffee. It did have a funny smell."

"Like burned flesh, Maribeth?"

"I'm sure it had that same unforgettable odor."

Ben pulled Maribeth's head back down to his shoulder. He gently kissed the top of her head. "You're safe now, my sweet. When I think that you could have been killed . . ."

They were both quiet for a moment, each considering what might have been.

Ben finally spoke. "Maribeth, why would a sixteen-year-old boy kill his own parents?"

"Jealousy. He was jealous of his half brother. He felt cheated, denied, put down because he had to stay and work on the farm, which he considered beneath him. Bernie was older, he could come and go pretty much as he pleased, he did nominal farm work, mainly took vegetables to market, but he had his boxing career, was doing well in that. All that, plus young Louis was envious to the point of murder by being made to feel less than his peers, Harry and Lee. So you might say, Ben, that he was very jealous of his half brother and envious of his classmates. It probably seemed to him that everyone was conspiring to keep him from what he wanted—to be who he wanted to be and to have his own identity. It was crazy, all mixed up in his mind, but those feelings led to quiet rage, which led to murder."

As usual, remnants of a Chinese meal were spread out on the coffee table in front of the couch where Ben and Maribeth were seated. Gently, he pulled her close to him and kissed the top of her forehead.

"So now, Miss Trumbull, are you going to stick to nursing? No more detective work?" Ben teased.

Maribeth nodded. Satisfied to be safe in Ben's arms, she raised her face to meet his firm lips with a kiss. The clean, masculine scent of his aftershave lotion and the strength she felt from his protective arms made her realize how lucky she really was.

"Yes, Ben, nursing is my only career from now on, I promise. That is, until we get married."

"That's all I want to hear, my love," Ben said soberly as he returned her kiss.

Oh God, yes, Maribeth thought, *nursing and marriage to Ben will be all I want in my future, always.... that is, unless someone challenges me, dares me to do something they think I cannot accomplish. I'd have to prove them wrong.*

She turned in Ben's arms as he reached to pull her closer into his embrace. He moaned with contentment as she responded to his firm kisses.

"I love you so much, Maribeth. Tell me you feel the same about me."

"Oh, Ben, of course I love you," she teased lightly. But as he fixed his eyes on her face, her voice took on a serious tone. "I'll always love you. Don't you know you're the man of my dreams?"

"Better stay that way, too. Honey, I couldn't bear

to have anything happen to you!" He squeezed her in a fierce hug. "So, miss, no more chasing after mysteries, eh? Promise?"

"I do."

Then he pulled her close to him, wrapped his arms around her. She felt the strong warmth that emanated from his body. She trembled in his arms, thinking how close she had come to losing her life. She held his face between her hands as she received his kisses. This was the man she trusted. This man never betrayed her, never faulted her, and she realized that in her stubborn independence, her one-track mind, she had caused him many instances of intense worry.

She recognized, too, the innate strength Ben Daniels possessed. He stood for what he believed in, he had garnered respect from his fellow officers and his superior officers as well.

Holding her, Ben kissed her eyes, her cheeks, her mouth, nestled his face in the crook of her neck, mumbling softly, "Mari, Mari, I love you so much. Could have . . . could have lost you," he stuttered.

"I love you, too, Ben, I really do. I was so scared, so scared. Hold me, please."

She reveled in the warmth and the tenderness of his kisses. Now, at last, she was safe. She was secure. She was loved.

Breathing heavily as if trying to control his emotions, Ben released Maribeth suddenly and slid from the couch where they had been sitting to get down on one knee. He grabbed both of her hands, kneading his thumbs over her knuckles. When he spoke, she saw deep intensity glowing from his dark eyes and his voice was hoarse with emotion.

"Honey, I've been waiting to do this the right

way, what I know your folks would want . . . to properly ask for your hand, but I can't wait, not after all that's happened to us, not another blasted minute! You know how much I love you, want you, need you! Here, been carryin' this around for weeks!"

Maribeth stared wide-eyed as he pulled a small jewel box from his pocket.

"Open it."

She did and gasped when she saw a diamond solitaire ring set in gold.

"Oh, Ben, Ben, it's beautiful!"

"Not nearly as beautiful as you, my precious. Mari, will you marry me? Please?"

"Oh yes, yes, yes!"

Solemnly, Ben placed the ring on the appropriate finger and kissed her.

"Let's make it soon," he pleaded.

"How about the day after I graduate in June?"

"And that is?"

"June fourteenth is the day I get my degree."

"Great, and on June fifteenth you'll become Mrs. Benjamin Daniels! Now, I really have to talk to your folks."

Sixteen

As usual, Maribeth's father, Judd, and Ben went out to the garage to go over Maribeth's car.

As the two men went through the kitchen on their way out to the garage, Ben stopped to kiss Maribeth's mother on the cheek.

"Mighty fine dinner, Mrs. Trumbull. Thanks so much."

She gave him a modest wave of her hand as if dismissing the compliment, saying, "Why, thank you, son. Wasn't anything special."

"Of course it was. You cooked it, so it was very special, ma'am."

He patted her shoulder gently and followed her husband out the back door.

Clearing the dishes from the dining room table, Maribeth looked out the window and saw Ben and her dad. Today she knew Ben planned to talk with her father, to follow the old-world tradition of asking for her hand, although she had already informed her parents of her engagement. And she had briefed them on her involvement in the D'Asardi murder case. The D'Asardi family, whose fresh fruits and vegetables they would no longer enjoy.

As she told Ben earlier, she had left out her terrifying experience at the Concord farmhouse.

"I didn't feel they had a need to know," she explained to Ben, and he agreed.

"It's all over and you're safe, that's what matters," he had said.

That's when she'd asked Ben if he thought she'd be called to testify in Louis's case.

"From what I've been told, honey, his lawyer is pleading him guilty of killing his parents and he is using an insanity plea. Don't believe there'll be much of a trial. He'll probably be sent to Bridgewater State Prison for the criminally insane."

"And Harry Holtz?"

"He's liable for conspiracy to commit murder, although he did plea-bargain with the D.A., so don't know what's the amount of time he'll serve, but he will."

Maribeth watched the men as they went to the garage. Her father went inside to drive the car out onto the driveway while Ben waited outside.

Maribeth's heart beat a little faster as she saw the man she loved standing tall, strong, and certain of himself.

She was a lucky girl to love such a man and she knew it.

Her mother's words on that day when Maribeth had informed her parents that she loved Ben, echoed now in her mind.

"He's a very nice boy. Already I think of him as a son," her mother had remarked.

Sighing deeply, she moved from the window. It was going to be a new phase in her life after today. No longer was she Maribeth Trumbull, daughter of

MEANT TO BE

Emily and Judd. After today she would be the fiancée of Ben Daniels.

She took the tray of soiled dishes into the kitchen where her mother was putting away leftover food.

"Guess Ben's asking Dad...."

"I expect he is," her mother said. "Think your dad's real proud, too, that Ben would honor him that way."

"Ben has great respect for both of you." Maribeth picked up a towel and began to dry the dishes.

"Mama," she asked quietly, "when did you know that dad was the one for you?"

Her mother washed a few more plates, stacked them in the dish drainer on the counter before answering.

"Maribeth, honey," she said thoughtfully, "I knew that your dad was the man for me when I realized he made me feel special. The little things he did for me to please me and make me happy, the things he said to me, and . . . the *way* he said them. All these things and more let me know that I, a girl from New Orleans, was his beloved. When you know that someone loves you more than every breath he takes, that you are the only star in the universe for him, how can you help but love that person? And actually, he made me feel better about myself. I felt valued because a real good, honest-to-God man made me feel that way."

She moved from the sink to sit down at the kitchen table, still stacked with dishes. She looked up at her daughter.

"Have I answered your question, Maribeth?"

Maribeth nodded.

"Yes, Mama, you have. Ben makes me feel the same way and I know I am his beloved."

Her mother stood up and went back to the sinkful of dishes.

"Remember what I've always told you, child. There's nothing like the love of a good man. Nothing."

Maribeth was well aware of her mother's family's position in New Orleans Creole society. She had been told many times by her mother that the proud DeVries family history went back to the 1600s. A mixture of African, Caribbean, and European ancestry, the family was part of a society of folk in New Orleans and other parishes of Louisiana known as Free People of Color.

Whenever Maribeth and her parents made visits to Emily's only sibling, her brother, Bart, and his family in New Orleans, Maribeth became acutely aware of the legacy of the multicultural climate that existed in the Crescent City.

She shared that legacy with her first cousin, Jasmine. Both girls were the same age, looked so much alike people thought they were sisters. Both shared the same skin coloring and red-brown lustrous hair, a genetic marker from their European ancestry.

Jasmine was delighted when Maribeth asked her to be her maid of honor.

Maribeth's wedding was going to be the highlight of the DeVries family's visit to Boston. They planned to arrive in time for Maribeth's graduation from Boston University on a beautiful Sunday morning and remain the whole week after to attend the wedding on the following Saturday.

The women had completed their chores in the kitchen. They were sitting in the living room waiting for the men to return from their car inspection. Mrs. Trumbull had put a fresh pot of coffee on the stove and she had placed a beautiful pound cake as well as a newly baked apple pie on the dining room table.

"They're coming in now," she said to her daughter as she saw Ben and Judd walking by the living room window to the front porch.

She laughed. "Now that they've worked on your car, Mari, they think they're entitled to come in the front door."

"Good thing you made Dad put that sink in the garage so he has a place to wash up."

"When we had the kitchen remodeled, didn't see any reason why we couldn't put the old sink to good use," her mother said.

"Man!" her father's voice boomed from the hall as he and Ben entered the house. "Does that coffee smell good!"

"Everything all right?" Emily asked her husband as he took his seat in his favorite chair.

"Yes, ma'am! Everything is A number one with the car and"—he looked at Maribeth—"I said yes with my blessings to the young man."

Maribeth ran into her father's arms. "Oh, Dad, thank you. Thank you!"

He hugged her. Emily held her arms out to Ben. After their embrace, Ben turned to Maribeth, who moved from her father to stand beside him.

Ben's voice was husky with emotion and his breathing sounded rough as if he'd just completed a marathon.

"My promise to you"—he looked at Maribeth's parents—"is I will love and protect your daughter till I die."

Seventeen

Maribeth DeVries Trumbull was one of five thousand graduates who filed into Nickerson Field at Boston University to receive their degrees at an outdoor ceremony. The commencement speaker was Martin Wheeler, who had recently received a Pulitzer prize for nonfiction.

Maribeth sat with her fellow students in the section designated for those receiving a bachelor of science degree from the School of Nursing. Trembling inside, she could hardly wait for the ceremony to begin. Over a sea of mortarboards she searched the bleachers for her parents and Ben.

Finally she spotted them. Her father was waving the tricolored flag of Jamaica. Maribeth smiled and waved back. She was so happy she felt sure that everyone around her might wonder if she had been taking "happy pills." She couldn't help herself. She wanted to tell everyone in the world that she had reached her goal. She was going to marry Ben, the love of her life, and she had been offered a teaching position.

It was two weeks ago that she had been summoned to the dean's office. The dean of the nursing school had been most cordial and gracious when she presented herself as requested to the office.

Waiting in the outer office, she was very anxious to find out why she had been summoned. She was certain that she was going to graduate with her class, she had earned nothing less than an A in all of her subjects with the exception of a B in statistics. Mathematics was always troublesome for her.

Could it be her involvement in the D'Asardi murder? Could it be that the school objected to that? How many people at the university knew about it? she wondered.

She had wanted to appear as professional as possible when she kept her appointment, so she wore a black suit with a starkly white blouse tied at the neckline with a loose bow. She wore sensible low-heeled black shoes.

She had told no one about the impending appointment, remembering her father's sage advice, "Everything is on a need-to-know basis, child, and if there's no need, keep it to yourself."

The dean's secretary, a Miss Erlich, whom Maribeth had had meetings with previously, offered her coffee, but Maribeth declined with thanks.

"Nervous enough already, eh?" the older woman said, smiling at Maribeth.

Maribeth nodded silently.

"Don't be. I know you've been a good student. By the way, aren't you the nurse who helped the police solve that boxer's murder?"

"Yes, ma'am, I'm the one." Was that why she'd been called?

"Wow! Must have been exciting."

"It was scary," Maribeth conceded.

At that moment a buzzer sounded and Miss Erlich told Maribeth she could go into the dean's office.

"Good luck," she said as Maribeth smoothed out her skirt before walking to the closed door. Before opening it she turned to the secretary.

"Thank you."

Her legs felt like wooden sticks and her mouth was so dry she wondered if she would be able to speak coherently when she got in front of the dean.

Dean Hornby stood up quickly from behind her desk and walked around it to greet Maribeth with a firm handshake.

"How are you, Miss Trumbull?"

"Good morning, Dean Hornby. I'm fine, thank you."

"Good. Thanks for coming in. Please have a seat."

She indicated a chair beside her desk and Maribeth sat down, grateful to ease her woodenlike legs.

"Well," the dean started, "are you over the excitement of assisting the police with their murder case?"

Oh God, Maribeth thought, *I'm going to be reprimanded, not going to get my degree.*

She cleared her throat, trying to settle the nerves that bombarded her stomach, and even worse, she felt her face flush with anxiety.

"Yes, ma'am," she said quietly. "I believe I'm over my little bit of amateur detective work."

"As I understand it, you played a crucial role."

"It's kind of you to say so, Dean Hornsby, but I believe I'll stick to nursing. It's what I enjoy most. I intend to leave police work to the police."

The dean nodded.

"I could agree with that, Miss Trumbull, and that's what I want to discuss with you."

Maribeth breathed deeply as she watched the dean extract some papers from a folder on her desk. Her palms were sweaty and she could feel moist perspiration on her brow.

The dean looked over the paper she had pulled from the folder, satisfied with what she had in front of her. She folded her hands on her desk.

"As of their last meeting sometime back, the trustees of the university have decided to enlarge the enrollment of the nursing students. It seems as if the war is ending, thank God . . ."

Maribeth nodded in agreement.

". . . and it is expected," the dean continued, "that nurses returning from their military service overseas, most of them diploma R.N.s, will want to further their education and become degree educated. So, to that end, with an increase in students, we will need more teachers. I'd like to offer you a position as an instructor in medical nursing."

"M . . . m . . . me?" Maribeth stuttered, almost unable to believe her ears.

"Yes, are you interested?"

"Oh my, yes, ma'am, I'm very interested. Very."

"That's great. You've been a good student, an asset to the school, and I'm certain you will do well in this assignment. Have you given any thought to working toward a graduate degree?"

"Yes, Dean Hornby, I have."

"Good. If there's any help I can give you, you need only ask."

She stood and Maribeth realized that the life-changing interview was over. The dean extended her hand to shake Maribeth's.

MEANT TO BE

"Congratulations, Miss Trumbull. Happy to have you join the faculty. Papers for you to sign will be sent to you in a few days and you can mail them back to me."

"I will, Dean, and thank you so much."

She did not remember leaving the dean's office, the drive back to her apartment, only the voice in her head: *I've got a job. I'm going to teach. I've got a job. At last I'm going to be a teacher!*

Eighteen

"How did I get so lucky to find such a wonderful person like you to love?"

They were having a quick lunch in one of their favorite restaurants in downtown Boston. Ben was still working, but Maribeth was not and was free to meet him for a quick bite.

"When did you know, Ben?"

"The first time I laid eyes on you. Remember? In the emergency room at Zion Memorial."

She nodded. "I remember. As I recall, you brought in a prisoner with a fractured tibia."

"And I couldn't take my eyes off you. But you, you went on about your business, matter-of-fact, as if I weren't even there. But I knew, come hell or high water, I was somehow going to get to know you."

"You almost didn't."

"How come?" Ben wanted to know.

"I was going in on a special case, but evidently, as I was driving in, the patient I had been assigned to 'went out.' You know, he died. The supervisor said she was short a nurse in the ER. and rather than go back home, would I mind covering the emergency room and she would see to it that I would receive the same pay as when I did special duty? I agreed and that's how I happened to be there that night."

Impulsively, Ben reached for her hand across the table. Gently he caressed her knuckles with his thumb.

His voice was soft and husky with emotion as his eyes held hers.

"We were meant to be together that night, that's all there was to it. Meant to be."

"Maybe you're right, Ben."

"Of course I'm right. No doubt in *my* mind at all."

He tilted his head to one side, impishly, and asked, "So, tell me, when did you know you loved me?"

She didn't answer for a moment, staring down on the table. She freed her hand from his, crossed her arms in front of her chest as if she suddenly had to control her emotions. She knew Ben had a right to know. She had been so difficult when she stubbornly refused his advice, involving herself in the D'Asardi murder.

She looked directly at him.

"I knew I loved you, Ben, the moment you put your career on the line to support me. You stuck with me, even faced your captain on my behalf."

"Girl, don't you know there's nothing I won't do for you?"

"I do, and I love you for it."

He leaned over to give her a quick kiss. "Let's pay the waiter and get out of here!"

They headed toward the parking lot to Ben's car.

"What a gorgeous day," Ben observed. "Hope it's like this on our wedding day."

"I do too," Maribeth said as he helped her into

the passenger seat. He took his place behind the wheel but made no attempt to start the car. She looked at him, questions in her eyes. "What is it, Ben?"

"Got a surprise for you."

"For me? What? What?"

"I have the rest of the day off. We're on our way to Logan. Junie's coming home!"

"Ben! Your brother? Home from the service!"

"We're picking him up in an hour."

"Wonderful! Your mother . . ."

"Can hardly wait. And, my dear, you're invited to dinner at Mom's. The whole family will be there."

"Am I dressed okay?"

She was wearing a plaid skirt with a hunter-green jacket and penny loafers.

"You look great. Be the prettiest girl there."

"You're just prejudiced, that's all," she teased.

Ben drove carefully and they arrived at the airport in plenty of time. The plane was an on-time arrival. Ben was so eager to see his brother that Maribeth had to almost run to keep up with his long strides.

She watched as he scanned the uniformed men rushing into the waiting area to be engulfed by shrieking cries of joy from family and friends.

Suddenly Ben's face was wreathed in a wide smile. He yelled, "Junie! Over here!" He pushed his way through the frenetic crowd, his wide shoulders making way to the soldier whose face broke into a wide grin as the two wrapped their arms around each other in a fierce bear hug.

Maribeth's eyes filled with tears.

As an only child she'd never shared her life with a sibling. She was surprised by the twinge of jealousy that flicked across her mind. She had never had a sibling of her own, never had to share. But at this moment when she saw the undeniable affection each brother had for the other, she was angry at herself for her selfish thoughts. *What's wrong with you, girl? You've got your education, the job you wanted, and you're about to marry a man who loves you. Better get hold of yourself, no time for jealousy. Get real!*

She watched as the two brothers moved toward her. The resemblance between the two was amazing. They were both the same height, over six feet, had the identical slender build with well delineated muscles, same deep chocolate-brown eyes. The similarity ended with their close-cropped hair. Ben's hair had distinctive silver glints streaked throughout, but especially prominent near his temples.

Ben's voice reflected the pride he felt when he introduced Maribeth to his brother.

"Honey, this is Junie. Junie, this is my fiancée, Maribeth Trumbull."

Ben's brother shook Maribeth's hand in his and kissed her cheek. "Staff Sergeant Marcus B. Daniels Jr., ma'am."

Maribeth accepted his greeting with her own. She returned the kiss on his cheek. "Welcome home, Marcus."

"What's with this 'Marcus' bit, bro?"

"Think I was going to go to war with people calling me Junie?"

"I see your point, but even if I think of you as Junie, I'll try to remember you are Marcus. It's even on your name tag," he observed. "Staff Sergeant Marcus B. Daniels Jr. And look at all those medals! You're right, kid, it's not Junie anymore. Our dad would have been proud of you, I know that for a fact. Come on, let's get you home. The whole family's waiting for you."

"Can't wait to see everybody. Mama's okay?"

"Oh, Jun . . . Marcus, she's just fine. Ever since she got word of your discharge, she's been cookin', cleanin', waiting for her baby boy to come home."

"Know I'm goin' cry when I see her."

"We'll all be cryin'. Boy, it's so good to have you home!"

Ben's prediction came true. It was a perfect summer day. The wedding took place at eleven o'clock in the morning.

Ben wore a tuxedo, but he had insisted that Marcus, as his best man, wear his military dress suit. Marcus stood ramrod straight beside his brother as they waited at the church altar for Maribeth to come down the aisle.

Ben's face glistened from perspiration that he wiped away with a folded handkerchief When the organ swelled with the bridal march, it was Marcus who laid his hand lightly on Ben's arm.

"Steady, man, steady," he whispered.

"God! She's so beautiful!" Ben murmured.

As she advanced down the aisle with her father, Maribeth looked neither right nor left. She wanted to get to Ben, to be near him, to see his loving smile that warmed her heart, that tingled her nerves, that told her that he wanted her above any other woman on earth.

Then her father kissed her, put her hand in Ben's. Together they walked the remaining few steps to be married "in the sight of God and the congregation."

After the ceremony Maribeth's cousin, her maid of honor, placed a highly decorated brand-new broom on the floor. The couple linked arms and on the count of three "jumped the broom," an old African traditional rite that signaled sweeping away the past. A sign of acceptance of a new life and a sign of marital harmony.

When they walked down together this time they both greeted family and friends with smiles and nods.

The heavy wooden double doors of the church were swung open and both Ben and Maribeth were startled when they heard an authoritative voice bark a command. Twelve police officers, six on either side, snapped a salute to the bridal couple as they ran, Maribeth clinging to Ben's arm, to where another policeman held the car door open for them.

"Good luck, sir," he said as he saluted Ben, then closed the door.

Breathless and amazed, Ben laughed. "I can't believe it! What a send-off! What do you think of that?" He kissed Maribeth without waiting for her answer. He shook his head. "Unbelievable!"

"It was wonderful, Ben. Shows how highly respected you are, sir."

She offered him a shy smile.

"May I say it's respect that you earned, that you deserve? And I'm very proud of you, my . . . my husband."

"Sweetest words I've ever heard in my life, Mrs. Daniels. Would you mind repeating them?"

"Not at all, my husband, not at all."

Nineteen

Sitting in the first-class seats of a wide-bodied jet—the tickets were their wedding gift from Maribeth's parents (he'd insisted they spend their honeymoon at his ancestral homeland, Jamaica)—Maribeth and Ben were reliving their wedding.

"Ben, do you know what I was thinking as my father and I walked down the aisle and I saw you standing there, waiting for me?"

"What, sweetheart?"

"How handsome, how gentle, how loving, how strong and proud, and how lucky I am that of all the women in the world, you wanted me."

"Oh, honey, you're the only one for me, now and forever," he whispered before kissing her with a tenderness that spoke of sweet promises to come.

They sat quietly listening to the reassuring drone of the plane's jet engines.

The flight attendant handed out warm moist towels to each of the passengers in first class.

"Dinner will be served shortly. Would you like wine with your meal?"

"Chardonnay, if you have it. For you, honey?" he asked Maribeth.

"That would be fine."

"Chardonnay it is, sir. Thank you," the attendant said.

With her mind still on the wedding, Maribeth questioned Ben further.

"During our reception, didn't I see you and Peter Logan speaking to each other? What was that all about? I was a bit surprised that he could make the wedding, knowing how busy he is."

"He's a nice fellow. Down-to-earth, with no airs."

"I believe he had humble beginnings."

"Right, and has not forgotten where he got his start."

"So, what were you—"

"Curious, aren't you?" he teased his anxious bride. "To satisfy your questions, he was telling me what a gifted, perceptive, intelligent young woman you are, as if I didn't already know that! Then he went on to tell me that he was indebted to you and would always be grateful to you. Said you could tell me about it someday."

"He said that I could tell you?"

"That he did. So why is Dr. Logan grateful to you?"

So she told him about his father's gambling habit, his involvement with Harry the Hawk, and the discovery of the jar of cut salve.

Ben listened to Maribeth's story, shook his head over what could have been. His voice hoarse and tense, he muttered, "Thank God that's over, but I think there's one more act before we can close the book."

"What's that?"

"Believe it or not, you're some kind of celebrity."

"Me? Why me? What did I do?"

"Here, read it for yourself. This is from Captain

Curry." He handed her an envelope with the official seal of the city of Boston and watched with pride as she opened the letter. It was from Captain Curry informing her that she was to receive an outstanding citizen's award for her civilian assistance in "helping the police fight crime."

With her eyes wide as saucers, she stared open-mouthed at Ben. "I don't believe this! After his fussing at me . . . I don't believe it!"

Their dinner was served with Maribeth still stunned over the honor she was going to receive.

A short time later their trays were picked up and they were due to land at the airport in Montego Bay.

When the plane landed, lively reggae music came over the intercom system. "Let's get together n' feel all right," welcomed them.

Swinging his hips to the music as he stood to retrieve their carry-on luggage, Ben announced, singing to the music, "We're here, honey, let's get together."

She smiled up at him, enjoying the pleasure he was showing, eager to get on with their new life together.

They went through customs without difficulty, claimed their luggage, and were able to secure a taxi right outside the airport terminal.

The sun was quite hot, but not too oppressive, Maribeth noted, as they got into an air-conditioned cab.

"Pelican Bay Close Hotel, please," Ben informed the driver, to which the driver responded, "My pleasure, sir, right away! Yes, sir." Maribeth noted the clipped accent as strange but delightful to her ears.

The hotel's brochure offered everything and

anything a visitor to Jamaica could be looking for. Touted was the warm sun, white sandy beaches, turquoise-blue water, excellent food and drink, with activities of every sort imaginable.

The Air Jamaica airline with its vibrant colors of yellow and orange, the national bird, the "lovebird," flourishing on the plane's stately dark blue tail had already promised Maribeth the vacation of her life, and as they drove along the roads lined with bouganvilla trees, coconut palms, lush grasses, fields of sugarcane, she was overwhelmed by the scenery, which included glimpses of the beautiful Caribbean Sea.

When they checked into the hotel, Ben presented his credit card, signed the register, and with a quick wink at the clerk called Maribeth's attention to it: *Mr. and Mrs. Benjamin Daniels.* She smiled.

"First time, eh, sir?" the clerk acknowledged with a knowing smile.

Ben nodded.

"Congratulations and welcome to Jamaica. Let me know, please, sir, how I can make your stay most pleasant."

Ben thanked him and they followed the bellhop to their room.

It was on the second floor, consisting of a large master suite with a functional kitchen. The private balcony overlooking the white sandy beach contained a small table, chairs, and a chaise longue.

As they stood looking at the ocean waves, the murmur of the tides sweeping the beach seemed almost magical.

"Ben, it's just beautiful!"

"Like it, honey?"

"What's not to like? It's pure paradise."

Their next few days were spent sight-seeing, rafting on the river, climbing up Dunn's River Falls as the warm water cascaded over their swimsuit-clad bodies, exploring the countryside, banana plantations, and cane fields, visiting a rum distillery. Their days were filled with excitement.

Their nights, when they finally got to bed, were marvelous moments of adventurous exploration as they embarked on the sensuous travels that they had both yearned for. Maribeth had never known, could never have dreamed of the unselfish pleasure her husband was able to offer her. She remembered her mother's words, "Nothing in this world can take the place of the love of a good man." Mama was right, she thought.

The Pelican Bay Close Hotel was hosting a jazz and blues festival and Ben asked Maribeth if she'd like to attend. Several noted musicians were listed on the program and she agreed. "It will be a wonderful way to spend the evening, Ben."

The festival was scheduled to start at nine P.M. on the beach in an amphitheatre-like setting. Seats had been arranged around a large stage that had a colorful backdrop depicting scenes of Jamaican life.

Maribeth and Ben were able to get good seats, not too close to the stage, but not so far back that they couldn't see the performers.

"This is so exciting, Ben. Imagine going to a concert outdoors, balmy, soft weather, the full moon rising over the ocean . . . What a night!"

"Glad you're pleased, Mari. I so wanted our honeymoon to be special and give us sweet memories. I, for one, will never forget it. Want you to be happy."

"I am, Ben. I am happy."

MEANT TO BE

She looked at the program she'd been handed when the usher escorted them to their seats and noticed several familiar artists from the States. She watched as Ben checked his program, then touching his arm lightly to get his attention, she whispered, "And you, Ben, are you happy?"

"Happy? Happy? Honey, I'm so happy I feel like getting up on the stage, grabbing that mike, and telling everybody in this audience just how happy I am! Believe me, I'd do it, too, but you might be embarrassed."

"Guess I would, but if you like, you can whisper it in my ear," she teased.

So he complied. "I'm happy. Happier than anyone else in this world because you're my wife," he whispered softly. Then he kissed her ear.

"Message received, over and out," she quipped. There was no more small talk because the show began with a ten-piece steel drum band playing "Hail Brittiania" with a jazz beat.

Ben went out onto the balcony where Maribeth was reading a book she'd picked up at the hotel's gift shop.

"Mari, I'm going to run downstairs to the barbershop, see if I can get a haircut. Have to start work on Monday and I won't have time . . ."

"Oh, sure, go right ahead. I'm all set out here, enjoying the sun, the sandy beach, and my book. Take your time, Ben."

She raised her face for his kiss.

"Be right back," he told her. "Can I bring you anything?"

"No, thanks, I'm all set."

After her husband left, Maribeth settled back to read. Engrossed in her book, she almost jumped out of her skin when she heard a horrible scream as if someone had been hurt. She couldn't figure out the source of the scream; it seemed close by, but she couldn't see any untoward activity on the beach. She returned to her book.

She heard the scream again. Someone was in pain. This time she stood up on the balcony and looked up and down the beach below. Nothing.

"Miss? Miss? Can you help me?" a man's voice came from her left.

Maribeth turned to see a young man with a terribly distressed look on his face calling to her from his balcony beside hers.

"Please, I think my wife is going to have our baby!"

"She's in labor?"

"I think so. What do I do."

The scream came again.

Maribeth said, "Go in and call for an ambulance! She needs to get to a hospital! I'll be right over."

She grabbed her room key, shoved it into her pocket, and raced to the room next door, which the frightened husband had left ajar.

He was on the telephone when Maribeth stepped inside to observe a very pregnant young girl on the bed, her eyes wide with fear.

First baby, Maribeth thought.

"My name is Maribeth. I'm a nurse and I'll try to help you."

She took the expectant mother's hand, asked her husband, "Ambulance on the way?"

He nodded, speechless.

Maribeth realized that the young woman was in active labor and was beginning to start to push.

MEANT TO BE

Maribeth checked her watch to time the contractions. Another one was coming, she could tell.

"Listen—" She looked at the worried husband. "Name?" she mouthed.

"Abby," he said.

"Listen, Abby, everything is fine. Don't be scared. What is happening is quite normal. Now you have work to do," she said quietly and firmly. "When I tell you to push, I want you to push hard. A deep breath, then push until I tell you to stop. Your husband"—again she looked at him for an answer.

"John," the man said.

"John is going to help, too. Here we go! We're going to bring your baby into this world."

It only took ten minutes. Maribeth was tying the cord with a shoelace John had retrieved and it was at that moment the EMTs came through the door with a stretcher. No one was happier to see them than she was. It all happened so quickly. Mother and her newborn baby girl were on their way to the hospital and Maribeth went back to her room.

She showered, allowing the warm water to remove some of the tension she was feeling, realizing, too, that she was crying. She couldn't help it. She had helped bring new life into the world, an awesome experience.

She had finished her shower, dried her hair, and put on a terry cloth robe when Ben came back, excited. "Just saw an ambulance drive off. They said a young couple who had signed in a few days ago just had a baby, right here in the hotel! Came in two, went out three!" he said.

"I know. They were our next-door neighbors. I delivered the baby."

"You what? Maribeth! You delivered the baby?"

"I had to, Ben. There was nothing else I could do. The baby was on her way and that's all there was to it. When a baby is ready, it's ready!"

Ben sank down on the bed beside his wife. "What am I going to do with you? Leave you for an hour and you're delivering babies."

"Well, you do have to admit, it's an improvement over finding dead bodies." She grinned.

"Got that right. Guess I'll never know what you're going to get involved with, will I?" He laughed.

"Don't you think that will make for an interesting life?"

"You bet I do, Mrs. Daniels. Tell you what really interests me right now. You look most appealing to me and my next move is into the shower to get rid of this loose hair. I'll join you, Mrs. Daniels, in one hot minute. Don't move! Now that's an order!"

"You're the police. I wouldn't dare."

She watched him peel off his shirt, his shorts. She delighted at the sight of his beautiful body. The planes, contours, the muscles of his sleek brown body enchanted her. She dropped the towel she had been using to dry her hair onto the floor and the robe followed it. She crawled into the bed and waited.

She knew that the man she loved, her husband, her protector, her champion would return soon and together they would explore and reach for the sexual passion that would give them the warmth, the certain love that would always sustain them to face whatever came into their lives.

She closed her eyes, gave a deep sigh.

Maribeth Trumbull Daniels, you are one lucky girl, she thought.

Epilogue

"Mom!"

"What is it, BJ?"

"You'll never guess what I came across at the library today!"

"From the looks of you, son, I'd have to say something exciting," Maribeth said to her oldest child as she watched him, his hand on the refrigerator door, looking for something to eat as usual. Her heart thumped wildly in her chest at the sight of her handsome fifteen-year-old. He had his father's slender muscular build and was already stretching toward six feet tall. His skin tones were a melting cocoa brown with dark eyes that demanded attention.

"I've already made sandwiches for you and your sister and there's chocolate milk in there behind the orange juice. Help yourself, just leave something for Emme."

"Okay, right, thanks, Mom."

He threw a leg over a chair, sat down at the kitchen table, and reached for the sandwiches under a sheet of foil.

"Here's the chocolate milk. Now, tell me what you found out at the library."

Chewing furiously, BJ swallowed, gulped his

drink, all the while nodding his head at his mother, who stood beside the table waiting for his announcement.

"You, Mom!" He pointed his finger at her. "I found an article in the local newspaper about you! Why didn't you tell us you were famous?"

"Because I'm not, that's why."

She sat down across from her son, waited.

"So, you found . . ." she said to him.

"That you were some kind of hero, heroine, something like that, helped the police solve a murder mystery, got an award from the city. Wow!"

"How did you happen to find—"

"History class. Teacher told us we had an assignment to research and write about something that happened the year we were born. So I went to the library and asked for newspapers for the month of January, 1947."

He took another huge bite of his sandwich, followed by another gulp of his chocolate drink. Maribeth watched in amazement as her son ate. She was glad she had prepared a hearty stew for supper because even with the sandwich and milk, he'd be ravenous by six P.M., but she did not mind at all. She was lucky to have two healthy children, even though at thirteen, her daughter, Emme, was starting to be concerned about her figure and had nowhere near the same appetite as her brother. Maribeth tried to make certain her daughter received the proper nutrients daily without appearing to pressure her very strong-willed daughter, who also looked like a carbon copy of her mother.

"She's just like you were at that age," her mother had said when Maribeth asked for advice. "She'll be all right. Let her make up her own mind."

BJ (nickname for Benjamin Judd Daniels) pushed his empty plate and glass to one side, wiped his mouth with a paper napkin, and asked his mother, "How come you never told us?"

"Happened so long ago, and at the time I wanted to put the experience behind me."

"The article said you almost got killed by the murderer!"

"Well, obviously not . . . I'm here and you're here!"

"Oh, Ma!" Exasperation flooded over BJ's face as he recognized his mother's reluctance to talk about her past exploits.

Maribeth knew her son and realized that he would not let the matter drop until he was totally satisfied, so she was not surprised when he brought the subject up at the dinner table that night.

"Good beef stew, honey," Ben commented. "Really hit the spot on a cold night like this."

"Glad you enjoyed it."

She got up to clear the table.

"There's apple pie or Jell-O with cookies, whichever . . ."

"Pie for me," her husband said.

"Me too," BJ agreed.

"And Jell-O for you, Emme?"

"Yes, please, but no cookies, thanks."

"Got it."

She returned to the dining room with the desserts on a tray. She passed them out to her family and it was then that her son informed the rest of the family about his discovery.

"Dad, sis, I found out today that Mom is some kinda hero."

"What do you mean?" Emme asked.

"Way back, guess it was before you and Mom were married, eh, Dad? Well, anyway, I got an assignment, history class . . . we all have to write about something that happened the year we were born. So, I started with January—"

"But you weren't born until August," his father said.

"I know, but the teacher said the year, not the month, so I started with January."

"What did you find out about Mother?" Emme was anxious to hear.

"From what I read, she helped the police solve a murder mystery, got an award of recognition from the city, but she won't tell me anything else."

"Because I was young and stupid, that's why," Maribeth said grudgingly.

"Oh well, now, *I* wouldn't say that at all," Ben said, looking at his children. "Great pie, by the way, Mari."

Maribeth nodded her thanks. Her husband continued his explanation.

"I'll tell you about your mother's experience, but you must promise to respect her wishes and keep this family history at home where it belongs. BJ, now, for your history paper, the year you were born, 1947, the first supersonic aircraft was flown faster than the speed of sound by Captain 'Chuck' Yeager. And also in that year Jackie Robinson became the first black to play in the major leagues."

"Wow!" BJ's eyes widened at the information. "That *is* something."

"Now," his father said, "are we in agreement? This stays in the family? Not that there was anything wrong in what your mother did, but because we are

MEANT TO BE 247

private people and do not, as the old folks used to say, 'put our business in the street.' Agreed?"

Both children nodded their heads, eager to hear the story.

"Okay. Here's what happened." He looked at his wife, who gave him a shy smile. "You two have to realize that all of this took place at a different time than now. It was difficult for black people to obtain equality in jobs, housing, education, and you both know how your grandparents wanted the best for your mother. They preached that daily and your mother and I want the same for both of you. However, as a result of her upbringing, any time anyone told your mother she couldn't do something or that she wasn't up to the task, she would die trying to prove them wrong. Almost did, matter of fact," he said softly.

"Anyway," Ben continued, facing his rapt audience, "as you know, your mother is a professional nurse and that's when we met, at Zion Memorial Hospital. Anyway, one night she found a dead man on the steps of ZMH. The police were called—"

"You, Dad?" Emme wanted to know.

"No, not me. But when they, the police, asked your mother what she knew, she felt 'put upon,' you know, as if she knew something when she really didn't, but that was enough because right away your mother was determined to get to the bottom of the mystery."

"And did you, Mom?"

"She was like more determined than ever. She would uncover facts even before the police did, and then she'd tell them whatever it was that she'd discovered."

"What did you do, Dad, while Mom was finding evidence?" BJ asked.

"I was trying—"

Maribeth interrupted him. "Your father protected me every step of the way despite my stubborn hardheadedness. Even went so far as to face up to his superior officer."

"That took guts, I bet."

"Not really, son. We were not doing anything wrong and we were acting like responsible citizens."

"Mother, did you solve the mystery?"

"Emme, the police said I helped them, but I had a lot of help. It wasn't all my doing by a long shot."

"But how *did* you do it?" Emme wanted to know.

"I guess it was logical thinking, my knowledge of medicine, limited though that is, and pure luck."

Maribeth thought back to the frustrating days and shivered at the thought of her being kidnapped and that last horrendous day at the D'Asardi farm. If, for example, Peter Logan had not told her about his meeting with Harry Holtz and the presence of the poisoned cut salve, she shuddered to think of what might have been. Tears came unbidden to her eyes as she looked at her beloved family.

"The police commented on your mother's persistence and her willingness to involve herself in what they like to promote as 'community involvement,' and as a lieutenant on the force now, I know how important it can be for the public and the police to work together for the common good of every citizen," Ben told them. "So, you can be justifiably proud of your mother."

"Way to go, Mom," BJ said.

"Weren't you scared, Mother? I would have been."

"Emme, at the time, most of the time, I wasn't. I was just too determined to find out why the man had died. Later on I did have a couple of really frightening moments, but your father, bless his heart, helped me get through those."

Ben's face grew solemn as he looked at everyone.

"Let me tell you, if you haven't already picked up on it by now," he said, "I fell in love with your mother the first time I laid eyes on her and I was determined that I was going to protect her even if I had to give up my career as a police officer. I loved her too much to allow any harm to come to her."

Ben got up from his seat at the head of the table to go to Maribeth. She raised her face up to receive his kiss. He helped her rise from her chair and with his arms around her told the children, "I've got some reminiscing to do with your mother in the living room, so I know you two good children won't mind clearing up and doing the dishes." He winked at them and smiled.

"Come, my dear, let's relax on the couch in the living room. It's been quite a day, and we deserve it."

"Lead on, my husband. I'm in total agreement with you." Maribeth smiled up at Ben.

"In the current slang of our son, 'way to go,' honey. Way to go!"

In the doorway of their living room, he turned Maribeth to face him in his arms and kissed her.

"I love you, Maribeth," he announced solemnly.

"I know. I love you with all my heart, Ben."

This time they said it in unison.

"Way to go!"

* * *

Gran'mere Em, as BJ and Emme called her, was sitting in the living room of her house in Cambridge. The glorious rays of sunlight radiated through the large bay window where she sat rocking and knitting, always her favorite place for relaxing or, like today, having time to chat with her granddaughter.

"Gran'mere, I can't wait for you to finish my shawl! I love the color, it's the same soft light purple as my gown.

Emily peered over her knitting needles at her only granddaughter. Emme Daniels was a beauty, all right. She was almost as tall as her brother, about five feet eight, with a slender build. Her skin tones were a delicate mixture between those of her parents, Maribeth and Ben, resulting in a finely textured smooth tawny brown. Her smooth dark brown hair fell in attractive soft waves to her shoulders. Emily loved her very much because she saw much of her own strong will in the child.

She continued to knit. She loved the feeling of warmth and well-being as the soft wool and mohair yarn moved through her fingers. She could see the light purple woolen shawl draped seductively around the girl's lovely shoulders.

"I'm almost finished, child. Be done long before your big night. Who are you going to go to the dance with?"

Emme's face lit up brightly. "I'm going with BJ and his girlfriend, Fern Williams. *Her* brother, Clayton, is going to be my date."

"Do you like him, honey?"

MEANT TO BE   251

"I do, Gran'mere. He's so sophisticated and smooth," she gushed.

"First real boyfriend?"

"Um-m, guess you could say that," Emme admitted.

Emily Trumbull thought back to her own youth and her first liaison with a member of the opposite sex. She had been fifteen and one of the nuns, Sister Marie Gregoire, had taught her to knit. Sister Marie was one of the teachers at the Catholic school she had attended in New Orleans. Called St. Mary's School, it was staffed by Sisters of the Holy Ghost, all women of color.

It was Sister Marie who discovered Emily's interest in Guilliame. He worked with his father, Guilliame Sr., around the school. They were considered part-time janitors, custodians, handymen who worked tending to the needs of the school that the nuns could not manage.

Emily smiled to herself as the memory of the soft-spoken, brown-skinned lad with the brilliant black eyes that seemed to see everything, but whose quiet manners calmed people, came to her notice.

She and her roommate, Violet, were rushing up the front stairs trying not to be late for class when Emily tripped and her books scattered in all directions. It was he who picked them up, returned them to her with a quiet smile.

"Here you are, mam'zelle," he said with a slight Creole accent, his worn work hat in his hand. She was only fifteen, but she fell in love.

They managed to see each other after that but Violet's jealousy almost caused Emily's expulsion from St. Mary's. Of course Guilliame and his father were fired.

And Emily received a tongue-lashing from Mother Superior when she was summoned to the headmistress's office.

"You come from a family of generations of free people of color, my dear," Mother Superior told her. "You must not align yourself with a person not of your station and class. Besides that, he is much too dark-skinned for you."

Emily remembered her rebellious thoughts at that moment. *Don't care how black he is, he's my friend!*

Now an aging silver-haired matron with almost unlined honey-colored skin, she moved her slender fingers swiftly and surely as her creation neared completion. Her granddaughter watched the older woman whose diamond studs in her ears twinkled. Her soft white silk blouse and paisley skirt marked her as a woman of exquisite taste. Emme loved her and knew that Gran'mere was more than a grandparent. She was a confidante as well.

"So," her grandmother said, "I understand you and BJ found out about your mother being a heroine."

"*That* was so exciting! Could hardly believe Mother would do something like that!"

"She got some of that spunk from me," her grandmother confessed. She proceeded to tell her grandchild a watered-down version of her friendship with Guilliame.

"So you see, when my folks said I *couldn't* be friends with him, I vowed that I would do what I wanted to do. So as soon as I finished my schooling, I came north, met your gran'pere, and fell in love. I've never regretted one moment of our life together. Judd Trumbull is my shining star and I'll love him till the day I die! And," she said, chuckling, "you know your gran'pere is *one* handsome black man!"

"You're right, Gran'mere. No one handsomer!"

"And like I said when that teacher told your mother she should not take the college course, it was like throwing gasoline on a fire! We were all mad, but your mom was madder. Don't ever tell her she can't, because she will die to prove you wrong. You come from a line of strong women, honey. You still want to be a doctor?"

"Yes, Gran'mere, I do."

"Well then, you will. There's not a doubt in my mind. If that is what you want, it will happen. Meant to be. That's all there is to it. It's meant to be."

She reached for her scissors and cut the remaining strand of yarn. She shook out the soft, gossamer, light-orchid-colored shawl. "Here, honey, try this on."

Emme's eyes brightened as she reached for the shawl. She draped it around her shoulders. The soft color reflected the roselike tones of her skin as she blushed with undeniable pleasure.

"Thank you, Gran'mere! Thank you!"

She kissed her grandmother's cheek, who responded with a slight caress.

"You'll be the belle of the ball," she said.

"Think so, Gran'?" Emme questioned.

"Don't *think* so. I *know* so."

ABOUT THE AUTHOR

Mildred Riley is a native of Connecticut and currently makes her home in Massachusetts. She is a member of the Romance Writers of America.

COMING IN OCTOBER 2003 FROM ARABESQUE ROMANCES

__PASSION'S DESTINY
by Crystal Wilson-Harris   1-58314-286-X $6.99US/$9.99CAN
Jakarta Raven was never one to back down from trouble. Her determination to clear her sister of unjust charges puts her up against New Orleans district attorney Zane Reeves . . . and a sensual attraction neither can resist. Now, with Zane's future at stake, Jakarta must find a way to clear his reputation, even if it means heartbreaking loss.

__IF LOVING YOU IS WRONG
by Loure Bussey   1-58314-346-7 $6.99US/$9.99CAN
After years as a struggling screenwriter and the pain of a bitter divorce, Simi Mitchell has finally hit pay dirt—a major Hollywood studio has bought her screenplay for a feature film. As if that weren't enough, the man who's directing it—Jackson Larimore—is unbelievably sexy. But maybe Simi's attraction is more trouble than it's worth.

__THE BEST THING YET
by Robin H. Allen   1-58314-368-8 $5.99US/$7.99CAN
Fashion model Tangi Ellington has it all—youth, beauty, fame, and enough money to last a lifetime. Yet something—or more specifically, someone special—is missing. Until she meets District Attorney Steele McDeal. The hard-nosed prosecutor is one of the good guys—but that's the problem . . . because his latest case is against Tangi's brother.

__ENDLESS ENCHANTMENT
by Angie Daniels   1-58314-445-5 $5.99US/$7.99CAN
Keelen Brooks has been in love with his best friend Charity Rose since kindergarten. He never felt he could measure up to the standards of Charity's high-school clique, the Cutie Pies, or to a man like her ex-husband, Donovan. Now Keelen is ready to show Charity what she's missed when they reunite for their ten-year class reunion cruise.

Call toll free **1-888-345-BOOK** to order by phone or use this coupon to order by mail. ALL BOOKS AVAILABLE OCTOBER 01, 2003.
Name_____
Address_____
City_____State_____Zip_____
Please send me the books that I have checked above.
I am enclosing $_____
Plus postage and handling* $_____
Sales tax (in NY, TN, and DC) $_____
Total amount enclosed $_____
*Add $2.50 for the first book and $.50 for each additional book. Send check or money order (no cash or CODs) to: **Arabesque Romances, Dept. C.O., 850 Third Avenue 16th Floor, New York, NY 10022**
Prices and numbers subject to change without notice. Valid only in the U.S. All orders subject to availability. **NO ADVANCE ORDERS.**
Visit our website at **www.arabesquebooks.com**.